What a terrific read! Shay O'Hanlon i͟s̶ ͟ it with—she's got a big heart and a smart mouth—anᴅ ͟ ͟ ͟ ͟ ͟ ͟ ͟ ͟ ly and nail biting (often at the same time). The secrets, insecurities, and deep friendships in Shay's world all come center stage in *Blood Money Murder*—and we get to see Shay go farther than we ever thought possible for the people she loves. Well done Jessie Chandler!

-Clare O'Donohue, author of *The Someday Quilts*
and *Kate Conway Mysteries*

Crammed with action and excitement, *Blood Money Murder* kept me turning pages at breakneck speed. Shay O'Hanlon is one tough broad, and Chandler's latest takes us with her on a nonstop ride all the way to the delightful conclusion. Highly recommended.

-Alice Loweecey, author of the *Giulia Driscoll Mystery Series*

Jessie Chandler really knows how to take the reader for a wild ride. *Blood Money Murder* delivers suspense, snappy dialogue, fun, and the host of lovable characters who have become family in Chandler's Shay O'Hanlon Caper Series. Not that the author skips the serious issues that beset her mix of urban Midwest gay and non-gay characters. Chandler takes on alcoholism, domestic violence, morality and relationships, always with a touch of her offhand yet right-on-target humor. From the scary scenes to the laugh out loud moments, *Blood Money Murder* is fast-paced and skilled—and the ending comes all too soon.

-Lee Lynch, award-winning author of *An American Queer*

An emotionally-charged roller coaster of a romp jam-packed with hot pursuits, bumbling bad guys, and leprechauns. A sizzler of an adventure!

-Maddy Hunter, author of the
Passport to Peril Mystery Series

Secrets, love, crime, and family all vie for center stage as Jessie Chandler masterfully conducts her quirky ensemble cast through the latest installment in the Shay O'Hanlon caper series, *Blood Money Murder*. Fans of Chandler's work will enjoy seeing Shay and her loyal band of cohorts join forces to help one of their own, while newcomers to the series are treated to a rollicking introduction to Shay's world that's sure to have them reaching for all the titles in the series.

-Carsen Taite, award-winning author of the Luca
Bennett *Bounty Hunter Series*

Blood
Money
Murder

JESSIE CHANDLER

Bella
BOOKS

2016

Bella Books, Inc.
P.O. Box 10543
Tallahassee, FL 32302

Printed in the United States of America on acid-free paper.

First Bella Books Edition 2016

Editor: Katherine V. Forrest
Cover Designer: Sandy Knowles

ISBN: 978-1-59493-503-9

About the Author

Jessie Chandler is the Ann Bannon, Goldie, IPPY, and USA Book Award-winning author of the Shay O'Hanlon Caper Series and the Operation Series. She likes to make people laugh and she loves to thrill them, occasionally at the same time.

She lives in Minneapolis, Minnesota with her wife and two ferocious canines, Fozzy Bear and Ollie. If you watch Jessie's Facebook feed, you might catch a glimpse of their fuzzy faces doing something Jessie thinks is obnoxiously cute. She splits time writing and selling various items to unsuspecting conference and festivalgoers. You can visit her at www.jessiechandler.com.

A Shay O'Hanlon Caper Series

Bingo Barge Murder
Hide and Snake Murder
Pickle in the Middle Murder
Chip Off the Ice Block Murder

Dedication

To Pat, Gary, Betty and Shamus of Once Upon a Crime—for all you've done for the mystery community, and for supporting every struggling author who's come through your store, including me. It's booksellers like you that make the book world go round. New Once Upon a Crime Bookstore owners Devin, Meg and Dennis— thank you for your persistence and patience in giving OUAC a future. Looking forward to collaborating for many years to come!

Acknowledgments

As always, the birth of a book is a collaborative effort. First and foremost, I'd like to thank Linda Hill for her graciousness when I approached her at the 2015 Golden Crown Literary Conference to talk about finding a new home for my writing. Yeah, I'm not so good at spitting out what it is I want. Jessica, thank you for your patience as I struggled to get your emails out of my spam filter and for continuing to kindly field the numerous questions I always seem to have. And for putting up with my wonky sense of time. Sandy Knowles, your cover is absolutely perfect.

To my first readers, your suggestions, editing and thoughtful comments are invaluable. Somehow it seems like I'm always doing this last-minute thing, and you've all come through for me time and again. One of these days, I expect someone to bonk me over the head and tell me to knock it off. Trust me, it would be a well-deserved bonking.

In no particular order, thank you Devin Abraham, Genta Sebastian, Terri Bischoff, April McGuire, DJ Schuette, Lori L. Lake, MB Panichi, Judy Kerr, Rachel Gold, Ellen Hart and Patty Schramm for slaving through my words, encouraging me and for helping make me a better writer. By the way, this list isn't all-inclusive, and I apologize for those I may have missed.

Risa and Gretchen, I hope your adventures within these pages are everything you wished for. Well, you didn't exactly bargain for what I put you through, but with any luck you're laughing!

KVF, working with you is an amazing experience. I'm learning so much, and would love to learn lots more. Thank you for taking me on.

And then there's my wife. Betty Ann, I cannot begin to tell you how much I appreciate your support, encouragement and the occasional kick in the ass when I need it. I love you, baby.

Last but never, ever least my readers. Thank you for your support and for hanging in there waiting for the next Shay and Company Caper. It took a while, but I think we've found a home where we're going to be very happy. We wouldn't exist without you.

CHAPTER ONE

"Can I get some damn help here?"

I glanced up from the espresso I was pulling. An older guy, maybe six feet with wide shoulders and a stark white Donald Trump comb-over, impatiently bounced on the balls of his feet in front of the cash register. A threadbare gray sweatshirt and black jeans clung to his thick frame.

A shorter man of similar age, mid-sixties maybe, with similar antsy-ness, fidgeted beside him. If he tapped his leg with his fingers any harder he'd give himself a bruise. The poor man's crooked, bulbous nose would be at home at an Alcoholics Anonymous meeting. Both of them looked unnaturally pale. Hopefully they didn't have some kind of a bug—I had no time for that.

"Be right with you," I said evenly. It'd already been a long, busy Saturday, and I was a hairbreadth from the end of my shift at the Rabbit Hole. I so did *not* need attitude this late in the game. A pained sigh that sounded like a strangling cat came through loud and clear over the hiss of the espresso maker.

"Lady!" The Donald hollered, "I don't have all day."

I narrowed my eyes and bit my tongue. I handed off the espresso to my customer and wiped my hands on a bar towel. "What can I get for you?"

The Nose said, "We're looking for Eddy Quartermaine."

"Eddy?" Was that all? Good grief. "Okay, hang on."

Edwina Quartermaine, better known as Eddy, had been a neighbor and my mother's best friend. When my mom had died in a car accident, she'd taken over mothering duties and raised me as best she could. The short, African-American, sixty-something spitfire who preferred to wear neon and tennis shoes would do anything for me, as I would for her.

I hustled through the back of the café, down a short hall, and stuck my head past a set of French doors that led into Eddy's half of the huge Victorian that housed the Rabbit Hole Coffee Café and her apartment. "Eddy!" I bellowed.

She bellowed back, "In the kitchen!"

"You have visitors."

"Who?"

"Don't know."

"Be there in a minute. Thirty more seconds on these brownies."

"I'll let them know."

All morning long Eddy had baked cookies, cupcakes and now brownies for the grand reopening of my dad's bar, the Leprechaun. The Lep, located in northeast Minneapolis, had been closed for the last three months after a leak in the cellar led to the discovery of a body beneath the floor. Of course I'd looked into it, and my snooping around had evolved into one great big giant mess concluding with a near-murderous chase through an abandoned mental institution. The good news was my best friend Coop and I evaded a maniac with murder on his mind and my father was cleared of any responsibility in the death of the poor soul under his bar.

Now new concrete covered the cellar floor. The exterior of the bar was freshly painted, and various items in dire need of fixing were repaired. Tonight at seven my father was set to unveil the new and improved Lep, and his regulars were itching to return to their favorite watering hole. The timing had worked out perfectly, since today was St. Patrick's Day. Green beer was going to flow tonight.

I informed The Donald and The Nose that Eddy would be out momentarily. True to her word, in less than a minute Eddy emerged from the back room wiping her hands on an apron and entered the Hole.

"Where's the fire?" She stopped abruptly and her eyes widened.

I shot her a quick look, and the expression on her face almost caused me to overflow the coffee beans I was adding to the hopper. Some strong emotion chased its way across Eddy's nut-brown face, but then it was gone before I could define it. Then she rounded the corner of the counter and approached The Nose and The Donald. She said something I couldn't hear, and they all disappeared into the back.

Twenty minutes later, Anna, my evening replacement, shuffled in. Anna was a tall, muscular woman, a stellar track athlete at the University of Minnesota who was also the sister of my business partner and good friend, Kate McKenzie. Kate and I had opened the Rabbit Hole as a joint venture a few years ago. On a pleasantly consistent basis, we managed to keep our eight café tables filled and customers relaxing in the overstuffed chairs next to the fireplace. No one was getting rich, but we were making it work.

After a quick chat with Anna, I tackled the last of the dishes in the kitchen. Suds tickling my elbows, I was startled by an angry, raised voice. I wasn't sure if it came from the front of the café or from Eddy's living space. An indecipherable exclamation from Eddy followed.

The soup pot I'd been scrubbing hit the water with a splat and soap bubbles exploded over the edge of the sink. I took off for her side of the house. Loud discussions were not Eddy's usual discourse.

"Bobby, I said you two need to get out. Now." Eddy's voice was uncharacteristically high-pitched.

I stormed into Eddy's kitchen. "What's going on?"

Three heads whipped toward me.

"Nothing, child," Eddy said, although the look on her face negated her words. "These two were just leaving."

The Nose tossed a picture on the table, a framed, candid shot of Eddy and me taken the previous summer during a barbeque in our backyard. The photo was usually kept in the living room on a side table. In the shot, I smiled with delight into the camera. Eddy gazed at me with the look an elder gives someone they obviously cherish. I'd just won a watermelon seed-spitting contest against my best friend Coop and my brown-eyed, pony-tailed partner JT. I was giddy, happy, baked by the sun and buzzing with too many beers.

The Donald said, "We'll talk about this later. Come on, Sheets."

Out the back door, Sheets trailed The Donald, who, by process of elimination, was Bobby. Through the window I watched them follow the patio-stone walk to the gate, let themselves out and disappear down the alley.

"What was that all about?" I reached for an appropriately green-colored cupcake cooling on a rack on the kitchen table.

"No, you don't." Before I could yank my fingers away, Eddy cracked my knuckles with a wooden spoon.

"Ow!" I jerked my hand back. Her aim was deadly.

"Those are for tonight. I let you have one and before I know it you'll have cleaned me out."

She was probably right. I asked again, "So what did those yahoos want?"

Eddy peered through the oven door. "Nothing you need to worry about, child. Just a couple of useless, no-good poops."

I raised my brows. "No-good poops, huh?" Both men rubbed me the wrong way but it could be that I still felt touchy about their less-than-stellar behavior upon arrival at the Rabbit Hole.

"Poops." Eddy nodded once but emphatically. "In my wild and crazy youth, I found myself mixed up with what polite society might call a questionable crowd. Which included these two ding-a-lings. They think I have something they want. Which I don't."

Eddy's youthful devious dealings? Right. Eddy was the straightest shooter I knew. My cell went off, blaring JT's ringtone before I had a chance to respond. I'd been waiting all day to hear whether or not she'd be able to make the evening's festivities.

Along with being my partner, JT Bordeaux was a Minneapolis homicide detective, and for the last three weeks she'd been loaned out on special assignment working some hush-hush case on a drug task force. As far as I knew, she was currently sitting somewhere on a stakeout where she'd been for the past thirty-six hours. She'd finally come home yesterday morning, scored four hours sleep, and dragged herself back to work.

"Tell me some good news," I said to her as I waved at Eddy and headed back to the Rabbit Hole.

"I'm sorry, Shay. With the budget cuts, we're short on personnel, and this thing is about to blow wide open."

"It's okay, babe." Not unexpected, but not what I wanted to hear. I understood the demands of JT's job, but that didn't mean I had to like them. "I'll save you some dessert. Eddy's been baking all day long. Speaking of Eddy, you should've seen these two bozos who just dropped in to talk to her. Rude jerks. They kind of reminded me of Jack Lemmon and Walter Matthau from *Grumpy Old Men*."

"Really?" JT laughed. "I'm surprised Eddy didn't pull her Whacker and give them a tap. What was up with them?"

"Not sure. They thought she had something of theirs. She doesn't. They left."

"Huh. Okay. Can you pick Lisa up on your way over? I told her I'd grab her about four."

Lisa Vecoli was my newly found half-sister. She'd appeared on the scene three months ago looking for a man named Pete O'Hanlon at the request of her recently deceased mom. She wasn't sure if my dad was the correct Pete she was looking for, but it turned out he sure as hell was.

After my mother died, seeking solace, he'd had a brief dalliance with one of the servers at his bar. She'd left and he never saw her again. What he didn't know was that she'd left with a little more than either one of them had bargained for.

Now I had a sister I really wasn't sure I wanted. We did have some remarkable similarities, mostly in our sometimes-explosive personalities. We were both angular, but Lisa was taller than my five foot-eight. My hair was black and short, Lisa a longhaired blonde. We both possessed the same strong chin with the same dent in the middle as our father.

That's where the similarities ended. In three short months Lisa'd managed to wrap my homophobic father around her lesbian pinkie finger. For years my dad and I had butted heads over my sexuality. Only in the last year, when he realized I was serious about JT, had he started to come around. I'd spent almost fifteen years banging my head against his anti-gay wall, and my head still hurt. I admitted to feeling just a tad resentful when he immediately accepted Lisa with the open arms I felt I'd always deserved.

These days, all my father talked about was Lisa. I ground my teeth a little harder each time he'd tell me, "Lisa fixed this," or "Lisa bought new chairs for the Leprechaun," or "Lisa came and took the old man out for lunch."

Yes, I'd taken a full week off from the Rabbit Hole and painted the Lep's exterior, but I couldn't afford to be away any longer. I couldn't compete with someone who was in school and had the extra time and energy to do all the things my father bragged about.

Okay, if I were to be perfectly honest, I wasn't just a little resentful. I was pissed off. I knew I shouldn't feel this way—it wasn't Lisa's fault my father fawned over her. I managed to keep my envy-filled thoughts to myself most of the time, but occasionally some snarky comment snuck between my tightly clenched teeth.

Today was a very big deal for my dad, and I was determined to keep my mouth shut and put a smile on my face. If I needed to play nice and pick up Lisa, I would do it.

"Yeah. If I have to."

"Thanks. I owe you one. Sorry to run, but I gotta go."

The story of my lover's life. "Call when you can. Love you."

"Love you too."

I headed back to the kitchen. Once the dishes were finished, I needed to make sure everything was packed and ready to haul over to the Lep. I'd picked up three rolls of green crepe paper and a bunch of balloons. As a reopening and so-glad-you-recovered gift for my dad, I'd also framed a poster-sized photo of the Leprechaun, which, freshly painted, was looking proud once again. He'd been wounded in January when the son of his ex-best friend shot him point blank in the abdomen. Thankfully, no major organs were hit. My father healed fast and was almost back to his old self.

Of course Lisa visited him in the hospital every day while I'd been tied up with work. She'd taken the lead on getting him to physical therapy and various doctors' appointments, too. I'd managed to paint the bar's exterior, and that was about the extent of my contribution.

Jesus. I really needed to let go of these suck-ass emotions. They weren't doing me, or Lisa and certainly not my father, a bit of good. Every time I promised myself that I'd stop blowing things out of proportion, Lisa did something nice, and I couldn't help but pop a gasket. I usually managed to hold the meltdown back until I was far, far away, but the by-product was that I'd become stiff and uncomfortable around her. JT and my oldest friend, Coop, tried numerous times to talk me down, but I was a stubborn cuss. Just like my old man.

The grand reopening was scheduled for seven. Two and a half hours should give us plenty of time to transform the Leprechaun. I gathered the decorations I'd bought and loaded them into my Escape, which was parked at the curb in front of the café.

Then I checked in with Eddy. She'd baked eight tins of brownies and six pans of cupcakes. She handed me the goods and told me to skedaddle because Rocky and his wife, Tulip, would help her with the rest.

Both Rocky and Tulip were mentally challenged geniuses that lived in my old apartment above the Hole. Rocky had come into our lives a little more than a year and a half ago. He'd helped prove Coop hadn't murdered his boss with a great big bronzed bingo dauber, and along the way had been absorbed into the family.

Rocky was a savant-like Rainman, a munchkin whose rotund belly tented his shirts over skinny, bowed legs. He was quirky, kind and always wore an aviator hat no matter the temperature.

Rocky had met Tulip in New Orleans not long after the bingo dauber trauma, and he fell head over heels. She was a cheerful, curvy, dark-skinned Creole who'd made her living busking balloon animals on the streets of the Big Easy. Rocky wooed her via Facebook, and eventually she moved up to Minneapolis to hawk her inflatables at kids' birthday parties. The two were hitched in a clown-themed wedding a few months ago. Yeah. Clown-themed. But that's a story for another day. Anyway, the two of them had this uncanny ability to pop up out of nowhere, and occasionally their sudden appearances nearly gave me a coronary. I had a sneaking suspicion one or both had bionic hearing.

Today Tulip's curly red hair was gathered in two braids that stuck out from the sides of her head. I thought they bore a remarkable resemblance to the horns on Bullwinkle the Moose's head. She was the balm that calmed even the most agitated person—a real-life people whisperer. Tulip and Rocky were perfect together.

I made it to my ride, a not-so-late-model Ford Escape, without dumping my load of desserts and took a peek in one of the cake pans. Eddy had decorated the cupcakes with green frosting and tiny shamrocks. I wasn't surprised she'd take the time to add that little special something. Eddy was that kind of person, always looking out for my father and me. I fought off the temptation to grab one.

* * *

Lisa lived in the Whittier neighborhood of Minneapolis above Eddy's favorite mystery bookstore, Once Upon a Crime. The owners, Pat and Gary, grinned gleefully every time Eddy graced their doorstep. Eddy grinned gleefully at the hard-to-find treasures she dug up in the Annex, a magical set of rooms where rare first editions and hard-to-find mysteries resided. Eddy had heard Lisa was looking for a new place to rent, and found her the apartment when she'd dropped into the bookstore a few weeks ago.

I pulled to the curb on Garfield and idled the car in front of the lobby door. Promptly at four o'clock, Lisa emerged from the building toting a colorful gift bag. She came to an abrupt and comical stop when she realized it was me picking her up instead of JT.

Initially, before I found out we were related, I'd thought she was a pretty good-looking chick. She'd fit right in with the Amazons, or maybe, more accurately, with a band of biker-Xenas. Straight, golden hair hung down past the middle of her back, and she had the same short fuse I did. Lisa was partial to blue jeans, black leather jackets and Harley Davidsons. Now that we were related, any theoretical attraction was gone, replaced with constant unease every time we were in the same breathing space.

After a moment's hesitation, she gave me a nod and situated herself in the passenger seat.

"Hey." She slung the seat belt across her chest and clicked it into place. "Thanks for picking me up. JT stuck working?"

"She's still caught up in the surveillance they're running on some unspecified building for unspecified suspects performing unspecified nefarious deeds." I checked my rearview, pulled out, and headed north toward I-94.

Lisa glanced at me, one side of her mouth raised in a half smile. "Unspecified stress too?"

"Yeah."

We rode in an uneasy silence until I merged onto 94. I knew I should be polite. Eddy's voice echoed through my mind, pestering me to lighten up. So I tried out some small talk. "How's school?"

Lisa was attending classes to get an art degree of some kind. She'd been doing an internship at the Minneapolis Institute of Arts, but that ended when the second semester started in late January. I still wasn't clear on what she wanted to do with her degree, but it sounded like she was going more for the curator end than the creating end.

"School is school. Can't wait to get out and get on with my life. Another two semesters."

"You think the internship helped?"

"I know it did. The Minneapolis Institute of Art asked me to let them know as soon as I finish, and they'd see what was available. I might start off dusting artwork, but it's a foot in the door."

I had to give her credit. At twenty-five, Lisa was seven years younger than me, and she still held onto the youthful "nothing's going to stand in my way" mentality.

We actually chatted like normal people for the next few minutes about college, jobs, the economy and spring, which was coming on fast. The snow had finally melted and I hoped we were done with the brunt of it. However, in Minnesota the potential for a snow-dump in March was always in the cards.

The parking lot beside the Leprechaun was newly paved and still empty. I pulled in and killed the engine.

"Shay," Lisa said quietly. The tone of her voice was odd, and I glanced at her. "We need to talk. About this." She waved a hand between us.

She was right. A huge part of me was appalled at my jealous and irritated attitude, but contrition always went right out the door when my father started reciting Lisa's growing list of glowing accomplishments. Somehow, I needed to get past this. Maybe now was the time.

"Okay." I gripped the wheel hard enough my knuckles turned white. "You're right. I've been an ass."

A dimple popped on Lisa's cheek and she laughed. "I wouldn't go that far. But this—thing—between the two of us has made it harder for everyone. I never asked for any of it, Shay." It was her turn to look out the window. "I never asked for my birth father to come into my life."

The windshield had thousands of minute pits I'd never noticed before. Why were small, weird things so mesmerizing when one was having a conversation in which one didn't want to participate? I heaved an exasperated sigh. "I know you didn't. And I know the assumptions I made when you first showed up looking for my father—*our* father," I amended, "were wrong. I'm not usually the kind of person that holds grudges." After a second, I added, "That aren't deserved."

Lisa didn't know how my father had reacted to my coming out, wasn't aware of the many years of fights and tears and fury that followed. She'd need to understand that for my overreactions to make any sense. I wasn't sure if I was ready to go there right now.

The other problem was that she and I were entirely too similar. We both thought we were right, and our stubborn personalities made it far easier to bang heads than to compromise. A part of me felt betrayed by both my father and by Lisa, although she didn't have anything to do with it except for the fact she existed.

I inhaled slow and deep. What the hell. "When I told Pete," I could not bring myself to embrace the "our father" thing again, "that I was a lesbian, he didn't hit the roof. He blew right through it. I've never seen him so angry. I was nineteen, a freshman in college. Good thing I was living in a dorm, because he kicked me out of the house." I laughed but the sound came out a bitter bark. "I should say he kicked me out of the apartment above the Lep.

"Anyway, I can go into it in painful detail some other time, preferably when I'm lubed up with a lot of alcohol." I rubbed a hand over my eyes. Bone-deep weariness settled like a shroud. "Bottom line, I guess, is that I resent how he's welcomed you with open arms when it took me a decade and a half to get to the point where he looks at me, *really* looks at me, without disgust on his face. I never doubted he loved me, but for a long time I wasn't sure he liked me."

The look on Lisa's face was cautiously sympathetic. "That's harsh."

"He winds up with two gay kids, and when he finds out about the second one, he doesn't even twitch."

"I'm so sorry, Shay. Now it makes sense why you feel the way you do. But please…" She reached over to touch me but stopped before making contact. "Know I'm not here to take anyone, or anything, away from you." Lisa sucked in her own calming breath while I studied the dashboard.

"So," she said hesitantly, "what do you want? Do you want me to leave?"

Was that what I wanted? To deny family to someone who carried the same blood I did? To push a sister away—a sister I hadn't known about? Lisa's mother had died not long ago, and what would Lisa have if she didn't have us? No. I didn't really want her to leave. I wanted the hurt and the resentment to go away. I wanted to get to know Lisa better. The only way that would happen was for me to deal with my own shit.

I met Lisa's eyes. Her apprehension was palpable. "I don't want you to walk." I blew out a frustrated breath. "The adult thing for me to do is to talk to him. Tell him how I feel when he starts waxing poetic about you. Maybe he'll lighten up on the over-the-top stuff. You and I, we're both hardheaded, used to getting our way. We're destined to clash, I think, whether we like it or not. But I'll try to stop before things go too far and we argue like a couple of hormonal teenagers." I gave her a rueful smile. "But I'm not always good at reining myself in."

"Neither am I. But I'll try and cool it too. I know I overreact sometimes and then off we go. If we get ourselves in a situation that blows up, how about we agree to apologize afterward?"

I felt a little lighter. This talking business was long overdue. Good thing Lisa had more balls than I did. "Sounds good. Thanks for forcing the issue."

Lisa said, "Let's get in there and give 'em hell."

CHAPTER TWO

The Leprechaun had undergone at least one name change in its forty-odd years of existence, but until now, with the exception of the memorabilia hanging on the walls, the interior hadn't been updated with the passing of ownership. The renovation was major.

Pictures of our family now lined one wall. My father had been a Mississippi barge hand, had sailed the Mighty Miss and other rivers for years after he'd gotten out of the service. Framed photos of vessels he'd worked, old shipping documents, buoys and oars, and other detritus of a life spent on the water occupied the other walls.

As part of the Leprechaun's makeover, each and every item had been removed. The walls themselves were still paneled in walnut-colored wood, but were now wiped down and nicotine-free. After a vigorous cleansing, every object was painstakingly replaced.

A friend of my dad's had come in with a huge sander and made short work of stripping and resealing the hardwood floors. The booths in the back of the bar were covered with new, sparkly blue vinyl and all of the wobbly tables didn't wobble any longer. The days of begging a free drink because it'd fallen off a cockeyed perch were over.

S-shaped track lighting was mounted above the polished, hand-carved, antique bar. Additional multicolored lights had been installed behind the bar and along the back of the shelving that held the liquor. It looked really cool when the settings were adjusted to flow from one hue to another and the shimmering shades glowed through the various bottles of booze. A huge mirror with an Irish leprechaun etched into the glass was mounted behind the bar and shone like new. It was one of my favorite pieces of decor.

New LED tape lights followed the edge contours of the low ceiling and along the dark exposed beams that ran the length of the building. Indirect, dimmable lighting could be set to the ambience my father wanted. Tonight, the place would be glowing as green as Irish emeralds in honor of St. Paddy.

A lot of the updating was cosmetic, but in the basement the retrofit was bone deep. Because of an unfortunate sewer leak, half the floor had had to be jackhammered and hauled up a narrow, steep flight of stairs and out through the kitchen. Old, rotted sewer pipe was replaced, and the cellar no longer held a funky odor. Now it simply smelled like a liquor store.

The other benefit of the deep clean was that the underlying, cloying stench of cigarette smoke was much diminished. If you took a deep breath in the back hallway or in the bathrooms, you could still catch a faint odor, but the cancer stick stench was no longer so strong that it knocked you on your ass the moment you walked through the door. It helped that my dad finally agreed to follow the smoking ban that had been in place for some time. He no longer let customers flick their Bics inside. Instead, he'd built an outside patio, and added mobile heaters to ward off the winter chill.

Snow was mostly melted, and now that the parking lot was paved, the muddy gravel and sloppy potholes filled with slush were history. Lisa held the door as I lugged the cupcakes, supplies and Leprechaun picture inside. She trailed behind, her gift dangling beneath a stack of brownie-covered plates that nearly came to her chin.

The bottles behind the bar glimmered varying shades of green, as did the ceiling. The regular lighting was toned down to a soft glow, setting the appropriately cozy and festive tone.

"Shay. And Lisa!" My dad's voice boomed from the corner of the bar floor, where he was hanging a string of cardboard four-leaf clovers. He abandoned his work and scooted over to grab the pans of cupcakes from me and set them on the bar.

Lisa deposited her burden and held out the gift bag. "This is just a little something to commemorate the day."

My father's face brightened. "Well, thank you, Lisa." He stuck his hand in the bag and hauled out a wrapped object about the size of a shoebox. "What do we have here?" he asked as he gave it a shake.

"Open it," Lisa said.

The wrapping was dispensed with, revealing a shiny silver case with a handle. *Pete O'Hanlon* was engraved on a raised plate on one side. The case thumped heavily when it landed on the bar top. My dad popped the latch and lifted the lid, revealing rows of various colored poker chips.

Lame. Nice try, Lisa. I'd given him a set of new chips just a couple of years ago for Christmas. Her set was a nice gift but nothing special. I tried to tone down the smirk that threatened as he plucked up one of the chips and flipped it over, then over again. The front and back of the chip were emerald green. Engraved on one side were the words The Lep, and on the other a miniature leprechaun pranced just like the one on the mirror behind the bar. My father oohed and aahed, and the smirky smile slid off my face. Damn it, she'd done it again.

He pulled Lisa into a one-armed hug. "Lisa, this is great. Thank you so much."

I tried not to huff as I hoisted the unwrapped picture of the Lep and let it clatter onto the counter.

The sound drew his attention from Lisa and her overly perfect gift.

"What's this?" He picked the frame up and studied it. I'd taken the picture from across the road one sunny day a couple of weeks before. The two-story building looked much like I remembered it as a kid with its cream-colored walls, kelly-green trim and heavy medieval entry door. On the second floor, the apartment windows reflected the sun, and in that moment, the place had felt like a long lost friend.

"Shay," my dad said, startling me out of my own head. "This is gorgeous. This your handiwork?"

"It is."

Lisa peered over Pete's shoulder. "That's a great picture. You really captured the essence of the place."

For no reason tears threatened and I swallowed hard. My dad set the picture back on the bar and tugged me into a tight hug. Rough whiskers rubbed my cheek as he whispered in my ear, "Baby, that's one of the best gifts ever. Thank you."

Guess I wasn't the only one choked up. I took a whiff of his Old Spice cologne and tried to center myself. "You're welcome, Pop. I love you."

"I love you too, honey." With that he cleared his throat and released me. "Time to put my girls to work. What do you think about playing with some green dye?"

By eight, the Lep was in full St. Paddy's celebration mode. The place was filled with the peppy tunes of a Celtic music mix and the drone of those well on the way to inebriation.

Coop hung out at the front door, carding those who needed carding. Once revelers made it inside, Rocky and Tulip happily doled out green bowler hats, four-leaf clover beads, cheap-o green-rimmed sunglasses and gigantic green bows.

Earlier, Lisa and I, along with Johnny, the bartender/bar manager, unpacked and washed my father's newest acquisition: two hundred pint glasses personalized with the words "The Leprechaun," and below that, "Nordeast"—in a shout out to Minneapolis's Northeast neighborhood where the Lep was located. The glasses were nice, and I wondered where he came up with the money for them. For as long as I could remember, the bar rode the thin edge of the profit/loss roller coaster.

Insurance had paid for the repair of the basement where the sewer line ruptured, but I didn't know where funds for the rest of the cleaning and refurbishing came from. Maybe from leftover insurance money.

True to my father's word, we were stained green from squeezing drops of food coloring into the bottom of each of those neatly lined up pint glasses. No matter how careful you tried to be, green hands were an inevitable consequence of the holiday.

Lisa and I came back from washing up, and Eddy and her best friend Agnes took over green drop patrol as glasses cycled out of the dishwasher. Lisa and I stayed behind the bar and helped Johnny keep the emerald beer flowing while my father schmoozed the crowd. Dad was a drunk who held onto his dry spells until he didn't. Then he inevitably took a spectacular header off the wagon and lost days, and sometimes weeks, in an alcoholic haze. Since he'd been released from the hospital in January after his gunshot wound, he'd abstained admirably. I was begrudgingly proud of him, but wasn't holding my breath for his sobriety to last.

I'd just exchanged yet another green beer for green cash and was reaching for a new glass in anticipation of the next order when a woman with flaming hair and a smiling face wedged herself up to the bar.

"Pam," I said. "You made it."

Pam Pine, JT's and my go-to dog sitter and all-around awesome friend, snatched a recently vacated stool and hopped aboard. On her head, a bowler with shamrock beads wound around its base sat at a jaunty angle. "I did. Your boys are sacked out at my place, taking up most of my bed."

JT and I owned two dogs, a boxer named Dawg, and Bogey the flunky bloodhound. The mutts took up plenty of mattress real estate, and I guiltily confessed to enjoying the extra room when Pam took them for the occasional sleepover.

I laughed and pulled a beer, watching the amber liquid blossom into Kelly-green joy and set it in front of Pam. "On the house. I appreciate you taking those goofy pooches over the weekend. With JT on stakeout duty and this," I waved an arm around, "it's nice to not have to worry about letting them out." I glanced across at the crowded floor. "It's going to be a long night."

She took a sip and licked green foam off her upper lip. "Never a problem. I love those munchkins. Go on now and help these thirsty patrons."

I did as I was bid.

* * *

Hours later I ushered the last patron out, flipped the lock on the door and pulled the chain to turn off the "OPEN" sign. Then I wearily turned around to face the wreckage.

Green streamers littered the floor, along with squashed hats, trampled bow ties and strings of beads. Empty bottles and green-stained glasses resided on every available flat surface including the windowsills. I grabbed a stack of unused napkins and crammed them in a pocket, too tired to put them away.

Johnny slumped over the bar, his forehead resting against the shiny surface. Lisa leaned against the shelf below the leprechaun mirror, her face slack, looking shell-shocked. My father was sprawled in a chair at one of the tables across from Eddy, who looked like she might fall asleep any minute. Agnes had hauled Rocky and Tulip home after they doled out all of the boxes of party favors, so they were spared at least part of the St. Paddy's Day torment.

Coop was the only one who looked remotely functional. He'd hoisted himself onto the bar and sat with legs dangling as he worked on a green beer of his own.

"Well," my dad said, "another successful St. Patrick's Day in the books." He blearily surveyed his kingdom. "Let's call it a night and I'll clean up in the morning."

I said, "No argument here. Lisa, you ready to blow this joint?"

She straightened. "Hell, yes. I can come in tomorrow and help you clean, Pete."

There she went again. I gritted my teeth and bit back a snarky comeback. I was scheduled to work the swing shift at the Rabbit Hole, so I wasn't going to be able to lend a hand unless I dug into the mess now. And that wasn't going to happen. I might be full of animosity but I wasn't a martyr.

Coop downed the rest of his beer in three swallows and wiped his forearm across his lips. Then he shook out a cigarette and stowed it behind his ear. "I'll come in and help too."

Irrationally, those words made me feel better.

"Cooper, I'll buy you a whole carton of smokes for all you did." My father's gaze bounced from one person to another. "I couldn't have done it without the help of each and every one of you. Thank you." I knew he would be doing or getting a little something special for all of us in the next few days. The man was a kind-hearted, if hardheaded, sort.

We embarked on the mandatory twenty-minute Minnesota goodbye before Lisa and I managed to break away. The ride home was a quiet one, but this time not because we were at odds. Exhaustion does have its benefits.

CHAPTER THREE

The eastern horizon was still dark as JT parked a well-used and sadly abused department-issue Crown Vic in front of her house. Exhaustion pulled at her very core, and she couldn't wait to crawl into bed and tuck herself around a warm, sleepy Shay. She had less than eight hours to sleep, eat and get back to the stakeout.

The Violent Crime Task Force that she had been loaned to was close to wrapping up a three-month drug sting operation, and she was more than ready for something to happen. Mexican meth was being filtered into Minnesota in record amounts thanks to cartels that were thrilled to fill the US void after the crackdown on over-the-counter cold medicines containing pseudoephedrine. If they could pull this bust off, it would be one of the largest ever in the state.

Inside, JT shrugged off a heavy jacket and unlaced her boots and left them neatly lined up on a rug next to the front door. Instead of a pair or two of Shay's shoes carelessly left in a jumble, JT noted a conspicuous lack of any footwear at all.

She puzzled on that for a moment, then went to the window to see that Shay's Escape wasn't out front. Maybe she'd parked in the garage and come in the back door. Boy, did her deductive abilities go out the window when she was this beat.

When she'd first moved in, it'd taken a while to stop badgering Shay about her general lack of attention to the orderly world JT was used to. Eventually some of Shay's laissez-faire attitude rubbed off, and the balance shifted. Now, JT lived dangerously and occasionally kicked off her own footwear and left them wherever they landed.

Shay was good for her in that way, JT reflected as she dragged herself up the stairs to the master bedroom. She'd become far less wound up about some things while Shay's scale of anal-retentiveness had shifted to more match JT's.

The day was brightening, staining the carpet at the top of the steps in bright streaks. To the right was Shay's office, and to the left the master bedroom.

The door to their bedroom was open just a crack. JT slipped inside and quietly closed it. The shades in the room blocked the light outside, and she blinked a few times as her eyes adjusted. As she pulled her holstered weapon from her belt, it felt like it weighed twenty pounds. She set it on the dresser. Too tired to even brush her teeth, she stripped out of her clothes and slid into her side of the bed with a heavy sigh. As her head settled into the down pillow, she tugged the covers up and rolled over to pull Shay close, anticipating the comforting form of her lover. Instead, her hand met cold sheets.

"Shay?" JT mumbled. She slid her palm across the mattress and under Shay's pillow in search of any trace of body heat. The pillow was cold too. Probably one green beer too many. With a groan, JT rolled out of bed.

"Hey," JT said softly and stuck her head into the absolute darkness of the master bath. "You in here?" Her heart started to pound. Louder, she said, "Shay?" Her hand fumbled for the switch, flicked the light on. Empty. Where the hell was she?

Exhaustion forgotten, JT grabbed a robe and checked the guest room and bath before heading down to search the main floor. Shay's shoes weren't at the back door either, and JT hustled out to the detached garage. Shay's car wasn't there either.

It didn't make sense. Shay had texted just before she left the Leprechaun to take Lisa home. Everything was fine then. Maybe she'd decided to stay at Lisa's, however awkward that might be. On second thought, Shay would probably sleep in a cardboard box on the street before she stayed at Lisa's. JT paused. When was the last time she'd checked her texts, anyway?

She bounded inside, up the stairs and dug through her pants for her phone. She pulled it out, thumb on the home button for access.

"Come on," she muttered in the seconds it took the phone to boot. When the home screen appeared, the message icon didn't indicate any unread messages. She touched the button anyway, and it opened to Shay's message from two thirty-five this morning.

Maybe she'd gotten called into the Rabbit Hole for some reason. Maybe someone called in sick. JT pulled up the Hole number.

Three rings later, Jeremiah, a trans man and a transplant from Georgia, answered "Rabbit Hole," over the roar of steaming milk.

"Jeremiah, it's JT. Is Shay there?"

"Hey JT—" The roar quieted then stopped. "Nope, Shay's off today after that granddaddy of a party at the Leprechaun last night." Jeremiah's drawl came through loud and clear. "Off the next couple days, in fact. I stopped by the Leprechaun last night for some green beer but didn't stay too late. Had to work this morning."

"Okay. Maybe she's at Eddy's. The doors open yet?"

She heard a clunk as Jeremiah presumably dropped the phone to check. A few seconds later he was back. "Nope. Locked up tight. I'm sure Eddy's still asleep. She was full tilt last night. Y'all know she's the beer pong champ?"

JT managed a laugh. "I did not."

"She was amazin'."

"I'll bet. I'm going to come over to the Hole. Will you have her call me if you see her?"

"Eddy or Shay?"

"Either." JT disconnected and tried Shay's cell. No answer. She sent a "where are you" text.

This was most likely nothing. Shay was probably sacked out on Eddy's couch. The thing was, Shay always let her know where she was or where she'd be, and JT did the same. It wasn't that they didn't trust each other, they were just that close. They exchanged casual texts between the two of them throughout the day unless one of them was unavailable.

JT chewed on that as she dressed. Was she behaving like a helicopter girlfriend? Was she one of those people who had to know every minute of the day who their significant other was talking to, texting with, chatting up? Someone who couldn't live without knowing where their partner was every minute of the day? No. She wasn't like that and she was almost certain Shay didn't feel that way. Did she?

Great. Now she was second-guessing herself.

She took the stairs down two at a time, jammed her feet into her boots and bent to tie them. Shoelaces in hand, she froze and frowned. Was getting dressed to go search for your partner a sensible thing to do when there was now—she checked her watch—less than seven hours before you had to be back to work?

Then she considered Shay's penchant for getting herself in trouble. Nope. JT's instincts had long served her well. No sense in doubting them now. Shay was most likely sound asleep somewhere, but she would feel a hell of a lot better if she knew where, and that was that.

On the way to the Hole, JT called Coop. After the call went to voice mail twice, Coop finally picked up with nothing more than a grunt.

"Coop, hey. It's JT. Sorry to wake you, but have you seen Shay?"

"Uhh." A long silence followed—then a snort sounding suspiciously like a snore came across the wire.

"Coop!" JT hollered.

"What—oh. JT. Yeah."

"Yeah you've seen her?"

"What?"

"Shay. Is she at your place?"

"Shay? Why would she be here?"

Oh my God. "She wasn't at home when I got in this morning."

"Maybe...she cleaned."

"Cleaned what?"

"The Lep."

"Coop. What are you talking about?" Silence settled, and all she could hear was a snuffle on the other end. "COOPER!" JT bellowed.

"WHAT?"

JT imagined his eyes bugging out as he tried again to shake the cobwebs. "Listen carefully. Have. You. Seen. Shay. Since. Last. Night?"

"Jesus, JT. Okay. I'm awake."

"Well?"

"Last I saw Shay, she was taking Lisa home."

"She didn't come over after that?"

Coop was quiet a few seconds and JT wondered if he'd nodded off again. Then he said, "I just looked out the front and the back. I don't see her car. Why?"

"I don't think she ever came home."

"That's weird. She was totally exhausted." He now sounded like he was firing on more than one cylinder. "Do you want me to take a look around?"

"No. Go back to sleep. I'll check Eddy's. She's not up yet, and maybe Shay went there for some reason."

Coop yawned noisily. "You sure?"

"Yeah. If I don't find her I'll let you know. I'm sure there's a simple explanation."

"Okay."

JT disconnected and pulled up Lisa's contact info. Voice mail kicked in and she left a message. Lisa was probably sound asleep too.

Just where I should be, JT thought wryly. She wanted to believe what she told Coop—that she was overreacting and Shay was fine. However, wanting to believe did nothing to stop her foot from pressing harder on the accelerator.

Eight minutes later JT shoved open the front door of the Rabbit Hole, jangling the bells above it. The place was filled with a nice Sunday morning crowd and a substantial line formed at the counter. Jeremiah and Anna tag-teamed the customers. If their smiling faces were any indication, they seemed to be in good moods.

JT stuck her head around the side of the espresso machine. "Morning, Anna. Shay show?" She knew Jeremiah would've given whomever he was working with a heads-up.

"Nope. But Eddy's doors are open now."

"Okay, thanks." JT skirted the line of the caffeine needy, and headed behind the counter into the rear of the café. At the French doors leading into Eddy's living room, she hesitated. The couch was empty of a slumbering Shay. So much for that. She tapped on the doorframe. "Eddy?"

Eddy hollered, "In the kitchen. Come along."

The kitchen always smelled good. JT took a deep breath as she entered the room. Somehow the familiar odors combined to ease the tightness she'd carried in her belly since she'd discovered Shay wasn't where she was supposed to be.

Dressed in Batman footie pajamas that bagged at the ankle because the flannel legs were too long, Eddy was sliding a pan into the oven. With a groan, she straightened. "These almost all-nighters might kill me. What brings you around this early on a Sunday? Shay said you were on a detail."

"I was. Hoping to get a little sleep before I have to be back."

"Well, what are you doing here?" As an afterthought, Eddy asked, "Coffee?"

"Sure. I think I'm out of sleep time anyway. Have you seen Shay this morning?"

JT watched Eddy pull two mugs from the cupboard. Over her shoulder she said, "I have not. Why, child?"

"She wasn't at home when I got there. I wondered if she crashed here."

Eddy poured steaming liquid into each cup and set one in front of JT. "She was going to chauffeur Lisa to her front door and then head home. Did you check with Coop?"

"I did. No go. I doubt he'll even remember I called."

"That boy does go out like a light when he sleeps." Eddy settled at the table. "You think Shay might've stayed at Lisa's?"

"Considered it for about seventeen seconds. I did try calling Lisa. No answer. Left a message."

JT picked up her mug and blew a stream of air across the top before taking a sip, eyes on Eddy, who had a frown on her face. "What are you thinking?"

Eddy blinked once, and then again. She wrapped both hands around her mug. "Might be she went back to the Leprechaun to pick things up. We left it a mess last night. Lisa volunteered to go in today and help. I could see that bothered Shay, but for once she kept her mouth shut. I do wish those two would either make up or agree to stay far away from each other. Might have to take my Whacker after them if they don't get their heads out of their derrieres." She slurped some coffee and fixed her gaze on the tabletop. "Truth be told I think it's Shay needing the head extraction more than Lisa, but that girl's got a temper too. Can certainly see Pete in both of 'em."

"The similarities in their personalities are uncanny. I'll swing by Lisa's place and then hit the Lep if Shay isn't there."

"Let me know what you find. I'm planting my fanny in my reclining chair and watching some *Criminal Minds*. Or maybe I'll try out that new *Scorpion* show. I think Coop DVR'd it for me."

JT finished her coffee and rinsed the cup in the sink. "I'll check in later."

* * *

Early on a Sunday morning, the streets in Uptown were quiet. JT cut off Lyndale at 25th and made a right on Garfield, which was a tree-lined one-way street heading south. Large Victorian duplexes in various stages of decay or preservation lined both sides of the street. Regardless of their state of upkeep, they were impressively huge. They all sported covered porches with decorative pillars in multiple styles, and in some instances a balcony poked out on the second floor.

Lisa's apartment building was at the far end of the block. JT slid the Crown Vic into an open spot about a half block before the apartment and hoofed it the rest of the way. As she neared the building's entrance, she caught sight of Shay's SUV parked on the opposite side of the street. Relief flooded her system, making her weak-kneed and somewhat embarrassed at the degree of her own irrational panic. "There you are, my naughty little buttercup," JT muttered. "Why didn't you tell me you stayed the night here?" Maybe hell had frozen over last night after all.

The postage stamp-sized entry was squeaky clean. Tiles in various shades of brown colored the floor, and the walls wore marble-esque laminate. Two locked doors led into the inner sanctum of the building, their glass panes print-free. The caretaker was taking care.

Two long, rectangular gray metal call boxes were located between the two inner entry doors. JT buzzed Lisa, impatiently tapping a nonsensical rhythm on the edge of the contraption as she waited for a response. After twenty seconds she pressed the buzzer again. "Come on, come on, come on," she chanted under her breath.

Three unanswered buzzes later, JT gave up. She pulled out her phone and called Lisa. No answer. She texted her, and then Shay again. Maybe they'd continued the celebration after they got back to Lisa's and were truly passed out. Now that fear had been allayed, anger began to bubble up the back of her neck, slowly at first, but it picked up steam fast.

"Fuck it," JT huffed. Irresponsible goddamn girlfriends. Might as well head home and see what little sleep she could eke out with what time was left. Shay was really in the doghouse this time. How could that woman not let her know she hadn't gone home after all? One call was all it would've taken. One text.

JT took the two long steps from the vestibule to the sidewalk. Her gaze bounced from the Modesto apartments next door back to Shay's SUV. Righteous indignation pushed out initial anger, and with it went the last of her adrenaline. How dare Shay scare her to death, and all the while that little shit was snoozing at Lisa's place?

She pivoted to make her way back to her car when something under the SUV caught the light. JT stopped, looked again. A silver container lay under the Escape's bumper. Green blobs dotted the pavement around it.

With a quick glance to make sure she wouldn't be run over by a passing car, she trotted across the road. The silver container was an upside down cake pan with the initials EQ—probably for Eddy Quartermaine—written on the bottom in marker. The green blobs were destroyed cupcakes. Now that she was close enough, she could see green frosting was smeared on the bumper and on the back hatch, too.

Those little shits. Lisa and Shay were probably half-plowed when they'd arrived, and, from the look of it, decided to have a food fight in the middle of the street.

JT snatched the cake pan up and stood, anger once again stiffening her back. She'd bet her next paycheck they'd made a mess of themselves as well as the Escape and the ground, and then had gone inside to clean up. Most likely they were passed out in Lisa's apartment. The only thing left to wonder was what condition they left the place if the fight continued inside.

The cop in her couldn't leave without one last double check. She slowly walked around the vehicle. Nothing appeared amiss aside from the frosted rear end. The doors were locked, the interior was in its usual state of Shay's version of organization.

The fresh wave of anger reignited her adrenaline. She pulled her phone out and dialed Shay's number one more time. The phone was ringing as she put it to her ear. Then distinctive, repetitive beeps indicated an incoming call. Maybe that was her wayward partner now. Was she going to get it. Without looking at the screen she answered, "Where the hell are you?"

"JT?"

"Eddy?"

"Of course it's me."

"Did Shay show up?"

"No, child. She's not here. But I need you."

JT had never heard Eddy's tone more serious, and that revved her recently diminished worry back up a few notches. "What's—"

"Don't ask. Get your buns back here pronto."

"Are you all—"

"Now, JT." Eddy's voice was flat. "Get in your car, stick the cherry on the roof, and skedaddle."

JT was sprinting toward her car before Eddy finished her sentence.

CHAPTER FOUR

Seven Hours Earlier

I pulled to the curb in a rare open spot close to Lisa's apartment. During the day the parking situation wasn't bad, but in the evening vehicles jammed both sides of the street. "Thanks again for all your help."

Lisa glanced at me. "No problem. I don't think I'll be able to move for a week, but I had a good time tonight."

"I did too." I gave her a genuine smile. We'd worked together seamlessly, easily anticipating each other's needs. With the exception of her "of course I can help" comment at the end of the night, I'd actually enjoyed myself.

"Oh, hey. Wait a sec," I said as I remembered the leftover goodies Eddy carefully packed for us. "Let me grab your cupcakes out of the back." I pulled the keys from the ignition to unlock the back of the Escape. I really needed to get the hatch release fixed so it could be opened with the key fob. Another item on my to-do list.

The night was quiet. The streetlights cast a soft yellow-orange glow on the mostly snowless asphalt. It wasn't really cold, for a northerner, anyway—maybe mid-fifties—but the breeze sent a shiver up my spine. I was glad I'd pulled my Rabbit Hole jacket on.

Lisa caught the last of my shudder as we met around the back of the SUV. "I don't know how you stay warm in just a hoodie. It's March, not May." She was bundled up in a thick, black leather motorcycle jacket with a black and orange scarf wound around her neck. Fur-lined leather gloves theoretically kept her hands warm.

"Guess I'm lucky that way."

I popped the hatch, and was about to hand Lisa's share over when something smashed into me from behind. My body hit the back of the SUV hard enough that the air was knocked from my lungs. The cake pan sailed out of my hand and clattered against the hatch. In the fraction of a second before my head ricocheted off the glass of the back window, I caught sight of cupcakes sailing through the air. Then my world exploded into sparkly white stars.

* * *

God, I was cold. Colder than I ever remembered being. It seeped through my jacket, through my jeans, leeching into the core of me. For the first time, I truly understood the phrase "bone-chilling."

I wondered how long we'd been sitting in the pitch dark, listening to the creepy creaks and groans of an ancient house above us.

My butt cheeks had turned into ice cubes hours ago. Probably hours ago, anyway. I had a hard time marking the passage of time in the dark. My head ached, and a rank, moldy-rotten stench made me nauseous. The wrist of my left hand was handcuffed to Lisa's right, and my right hand and Lisa's left were secured with zip ties to what felt like a lumpy, horizontal pipe running behind us at shoulder level. Maybe the lumps were rust. It was hard to tell.

Every time I shifted my left arm, hers was forced to come with mine and vice versa. Initially we sniped at each other, but as minutes bled into a timeless void we fell into a somewhat more forgiving rhythm of tandem movement.

At Lisa's place, after someone used my head as a ping pong ball against the rear window of my car, I'd lost a few seconds watching stars zing around—enough time for men wearing fittingly ridiculous yet utterly terrifying rubbery plastic leprechaun masks to shanghai, zip tie and stuff both Lisa and me into the back of a U-Haul truck.

The execution of the snatch was a thing of beauty— happening so fast I didn't even have a chance to yell before someone stuck a foul-tasting rag in my mouth and secured it with a strip of cloth around my head. Then they zip tied our ankles together too. Of course our abductors had the element of surprise on their side, but still. No doubt Lisa and I were going to have to turn in our butch cards after this.

Let me tell you, a trip in the back of an empty moving truck without the use of your limbs is not a pleasant experience. Between being thrown into each other and against the side of the truck, both Lisa and I were pissed off and in pain. I could feel anger radiating from her. I wondered if she sensed the same from me. Along with fear.

Who were these leprechaun people? They were similar in build to the Donald and the Nose who'd paid Eddy a visit. Eddy did mention the two men thought she was in possession of something they wanted. The leap from two old dudes ticking Eddy off to mask-wearing kidnappers seemed a little hard to make. Did Lisa have enemies? We really knew nothing of her past. Anything was possible.

What about anyone in my own past who might pull a stunt like this? Yeah, I'd landed on the bad side of a string of people over the years, but who'd care enough to do this? Maybe this was someone's idea of a really bad joke. If that were the case, whoever was behind it would feel my wrath because I didn't find one thing about it funny. Not at all.

Coop was involved in a group called the Green Beans for Peace and Preservation—a local, environmentally-concerned organization, sort of like a mini Greenpeace. They got into their share of trouble during protests. I'd bailed Coop out of the clink more than once. Some of the members were pranksters, but I couldn't see them coming up with something this obnoxious.

Which brought me full circle back to Lisa. She was the unknown quantity in this fucked-up equation. What did they say? The simplest explanation was usually the right one?

Eventually the truck turned off whatever road we were traveling and did a lot of bouncing and jouncing. The Minnesota Department of Transportation needed to coordinate a serious highway overhaul. After a few minutes the big truck rumbled to a stop and then a beep beep beeping sounded as we jerked into reverse.

The doors screeched open and for a second I was relieved to be delivered from the belly of the mechanical beast. Then I saw what was coming and changed my mind.

The truck was backed up to a storm cellar built into the foundation of an old house. Kids or weather, or maybe something indefinably more sinister had shattered most of the windows in my limited line of sight. The red glow of taillights reflected off worn clapboard siding, planks grooved and curled from years of exposure.

The cellar's angled doors were thrown open, and the ominous hole leading into the ground looked like a pool of India ink.

I nearly had a heart attack when one of the masked bandits came at me with a box cutter. But all he did was slice the zip ties securing Lisa's and my ankles. Guess they didn't want to carry us into that god-awful pit. We were prodded at box cutter-point down a creaky set of stairs into a horrifying, cobwebby, musty space.

One of the leprechauns propped a small flashlight, which did little to light the area, on the steps and pushed me face-first onto the dirty ground in the middle of the room. Behind me, I heard a very brief scuffle, but I couldn't turn my head enough to see what was happening. Lisa grunted painfully, and then she was on her belly in the dirt beside me. Moldy, earthy scents filled my nostrils. I bit hard on the soggy cloth between my teeth and concentrated on controlling my breathing. If this was how it felt to be buried alive…I stopped that train of thought in its tracks and forced myself not to go there. If I did I'd probably have a meltdown and that wouldn't do us any good at all.

Up to this point our captors hadn't spoken a word. As Lisa and I languished on that disgusting floor, a whispered argument broke out between our abductors. From what I could gather from the mask-muffled, whispered conversation, the problem revolved around handcuffs. They were supposed to have two sets but could find only one.

Their solution was to roll us back-to-back—which doesn't feel very good when one's hands are immobilized behind her—and handcuff my left hand to Lisa's right. Then they sliced the zip ties off our wrists. One guy grabbed my unhooked arm, the other took hold of Lisa's, and between the two of them they pulled us to our feet.

About this time I decided to try to escape, but my attempt to twist free was abruptly halted. Bastards.

We were shoved onto our asses on the dirt against a wall. They wrestled our noncuffed hands into position at shoulder level and zip tied us none too gently, to a skeezy pipe. One of them grabbed my hair and held me still while the other guy cut the gag off. I spit the cloth out and tried to demand an explanation but my mouth was so dry I couldn't speak. I tried to kick at the leprechaun closest to me. Unfortunately, his reflexes were quick. He leaped away and my foot only grazed his pants.

Lisa followed my lead and her foot struck gold, nailing the other guy square in the crotch. He backpedaled with a squeal, cupped his man-goods and fled, hobbling up the stairs wailing like a banshee. The other guy grabbed the flashlight off the step and fled after Mr. Balls of Fire.

A minute later the cellar doors slammed shut, blocking out what little moonlight had trickled in. Complete blackness settled over me like a living, suffocating thing. From the banging and scraping outside the doors, it sounded like they had secured them somehow to ensure we couldn't get out even if we managed to escape our bonds.

Assholes. To say the least.

I shifted again, trying to find a more comfortable position. Between the angle of my right arm and the sharp edges of the zip tie digging into my flesh, I was losing circulation fast.

"I don't think I can feel my hand anymore," Lisa said, breaking the smothering silence. "Goddamn it!" She thrashed violently for a second, then collapsed, panting, against the wall.

"Yeah, I can't figure out any way to escape either."

"No duh."

I'd been planning to ask her some questions, see if she had enemies, but her tone and her attitude was so pissy I kept my mouth shut.

The space was claustrophobic. Time ticked by one long, unending second after another. I closed my eyes and tried to shut out the dark, reminding myself to control my breathing or I was going to hyperventilate. Last thing I wanted to do was suck some unknown strain of mold spores into my lungs, and die before an antidote could be found. Now I totally understood how darkness-based sensory deprivation could drive someone insane.

At some point I dozed off. A shriek startled me awake. I added my own yelp as I felt panicked flailing and then a body land on me.

"What?" I blinked a couple of times until I realized my eyes were actually open and Lisa was freaking out.

"Omigod. Something skittered across my leg!" Lisa's voice was on the high end of soprano.

"Is it on you? Where?" I tried to swat my hand around but was moving at cross-purposes with hers and we didn't get anywhere.

She shifted from soprano into a whisper. "What if this place is infested with something?"

My entire body stiffened. I didn't like creepy crawlies any more than she did.

For the next few interminable minutes, we hardly dared breathe, straining for any sound that might indicate the presence of an unwelcome visitor. As time went on without an indication of invasion, we both began to relax.

I said, "Who are these guys? What do they want? You sure you don't know them?"

"Yes, I'm sure. Just like I was sure the last time you asked."

"Who've you ticked off lately?"

"Why do you think it's me they were after?"

"Well, Little Miss Goodie Poopers, we were at your place when they snatched us. Therefore they must have been waiting for you."

"I haven't made anyone angry lately. Except you. Maybe you're the one who coordinated this."

"That's stupid. Why would I do that?"

Lisa was quiet for a moment. "I have no idea."

"You know what?"

"No. What?"

"During these mini-arguments of ours, I forget how cold I am."

"Yeah." Lisa huffed a breath. "I do too."

After a few more minutes I said, "Not being able to tell if my eyes are open or closed is very disconcerting."

"Amen, sister."

Lisa inhaled sharply, jerking her right wrist, and my left, to her face to stifle a sneeze. Mist settled over both our hands. So disgusting.

She sucked up snot. "Sorry about that. I think I'm allergic to mold." She sneezed again, turning her head away this time instead of spraying me. She must've inherited allergies from her mother because our father had plenty of problems, but not that particular malady.

I giggled. This entire episode was unbelievable. Kidnapped a couple hours after St. Patrick's Day by two leprechaun-mask-wearing bandits? Who in their right mind would ever believe it? Lisa laughed with me, and for just a flash in time, things felt like they might be okay. She said, "Whew. I needed that. What now?"

A pall settled over us like a friar's robe, dark and thick and coarse. Frustration blended into anger, and I yanked again at the tie securing my wrist to the pipe. The sharp edge dug into my skin. "Let's pull this stinking pipe out of the wall."

"Maybe if we can get our fingers under it we'll have enough leverage."

"Okay."

"On three, we bring our hands up and see if we can get a grip."

Together we chanted, "One, two, three," and raised our connected hands. My knuckles hit the pipe, and I fumbled to slide my fingers under the metal. For a couple of seconds we tug-of-warred until we coordinated our efforts.

Lisa said, "I'm under. You?"

"Yup."

For the next who-knew-how-long we tugged and yanked and pushed against the pipe. "This isn't working," I finally said. "We need more leverage."

The unrelenting dark was filled with harsh breathing. Lisa said, "Let's try again. It'll hurt your wrist like a bitch but use your other hand too."

I took a fortifying breath and adjusted my grip. "Now!" We struggled to execute what amounted to a seated bench press. I was sure I'd have a permanent imprint of rough stone and jagged cement tattooed into my back right through my jacket.

My zipped wrist felt raw. As I was about to call it, the pipe shifted. "You feel that?"

"Yeah. Let me rest a second and let's try again."

While we recovered, I rattled the metal tube. Sure enough, I found just a little play that hadn't been there before. Hot fucking damn.

We pushed, we pulled and we wiggled that godforsaken pipe. If we'd been able to turn around and brace our feet against the wall, we probably would have made quick work of our project. Finally, thankfully, the pipe on Lisa's side broke away from the wall and she could move it back and forth about half a foot.

"You realize," Lisa said, "we need to crack the pipe in half or somehow get to a fitting and snap it or unscrew it in order to slide the zip ties off."

I'd thought about that as we worked. The pipe could have all the play in the world, but unless we severed or broke it so the zips could slide off, we weren't going anywhere.

"I wonder when they're coming back."

Lisa blew out a sharp breath. "Me too. Try again."

Five minutes later, whatever held the pipe on Lisa's end gave way completely. Not so for my side of the world. I muttered, "Come on, you son of a bitch." With a groan I slumped back, breathing hard. "The weakest part of this containment equation is the zip ties." I contemplated that for a second and huffed in frustration.

"What? Did you hear something?"

"No, I'm just moaning."

"I'm totally going to have nightmares after this."

"You and me both."

"I'm waiting for a possum to waddle over and chew our noses off."

"A possum? Really?"

"Would a skunk turning tail on us be better?"

"Jesus Lisa. Get a grip on that imagination."

"All right, you baby. I'll stop. Now, what were you going to say?"

"Oh." What was I about to tell her? The insidious dark was blotting my brain cells out one by one. "Oh yeah. I thought of something." The though returned in a rush and excitement forced my voice up an octave. "I can't believe I forgot this. The Leprechaun Loonies might've relieved us of our cell phones but didn't bother with a frisk job. There's a folding knife in my front pocket."

"Are you shitting me? Seriously? You waited all this time to mention it? A coffee-making, bartending, knife-wielding chick? Now that's more like it. Which pocket?"

Therein lay the problem. My left hip pocket was reserved for my phone, and everything else went into the right. With my right hand out of commission, I'd have to reach across my body with my left, and Lisa's right would have to come along for the ride. I explained the situation.

Lisa said, "Roll your hips as best you can toward me, and I'll try and pull the knife out. My hand will be at a better angle than yours."

I pivoted my lower body and grimaced as the tie again dug into my wrist. At this rate, my hand would soon become the long lost sister of Thing from *The Addams Family*.

The pressure of Lisa's palm on my leg felt reassuring as I tried to guide her to the pocket's opening.

"Okay," she said. I felt the light touch of her fingertips as she explored the denim. "Here we go." She slid her fingers inside the pocket and tried to push deeper.

I stifled a laugh and attempted not to jerk away. She stopped, and I relaxed.

Then her fingers moved and I tensed again.

"Shay, are you ticklish?" She poked me with a finger and I snickered. The more I tried not to react the more sensitive I became. God, I hated that.

"You *are* ticklish." She dug into my hipbone and I thrashed once then froze with a pained gasp when my movements yanked on the zip tie.

"Not...fair," I panted.

A smile I couldn't see danced in Lisa's voice. "Relax. I'll be gentle, I promise."

"I bet you will." I drew a calming breath and concentrated on not reacting. If someone heard us, they'd think we were about to have sex. "Go ahead."

After a few exploratory moments, Lisa asked, "What the hell do you have in there? All I feel is paper and some plastic."

"I don't know. Money and a poop bag or two. The knife's probably below that stuff since it's heavier."

Lisa crept deeper and I barked out another laugh. She said, "I can't go further. Can you scooch any closer?"

The evil little tie was too tight to slide along the pipe. "There's not enough play. You?"

"Some. If I can pivot my arm back and forth—" She held on to me as she seesawed her left arm up and down. After a few seconds she began to make growling sounds.

I flinched in sympathy at the thought of the back of her hand chafing against the rusty pipe like cheese shredded with a grater.

"Ow—if only this stinking pipe was smoother—oh!" Her fingers dug ever deeper into my flesh, and with a howl that echoed in the small space, she was suddenly perched half on top of me.

"Holy shit," Lisa hissed, her breath coming in short pants. "That hurt."

"Didn't lop your hand off, did you?"

"No, but I'll probably come down with tetanus. It feels like the only thing holding my wrist to my forearm is bone."

"You're not serious."

Lisa managed a shaky laugh. "I hope not."

"Hey, I could call you Lockjaw Lisa."

She gave my hip another shot and I involuntarily jerked. "Okay, stop," I said quickly before she did it again. "I won't call you that. I'll just think it."

"Oh, Shay."

"Back to the knife. Let's try this again, shall we?"

"Ready?"

"Go."

Lisa plunged deeper into my pocket. I steeled myself not to jump. Why was it when something initially tickled, the rest of the tickle sensors in the body came roaring to life? "Arg! Stop!"

She immediately stilled. "You okay?"

I swallowed an involuntarily giggle and took a deep breath, blowing out slowly. "Yeah, just…tread lightly."

"Okay."

She inched a little deeper, stopped when I tensed, and waited patiently until I loosened up. Then she moved again. "I've exchanged plastic and paper for round metal objects. Ready?"

"Yeah." I gritted my teeth and tried to will my body into a state of relaxation. Fat chance.

Lisa made it past the bend in my hip and onto the side of my thigh. I was about to dissolve into another uncontrollable paroxysm when she said, "I feel it." She gently pressed the pads of icy fingers against my leg. The cold seeped through the cloth of my pocket. "Relax." Before I could follow her directions she extracted her hand as fast as she could while I squealed like a three-year-old.

She let me go on for a couple of seconds then cut me off midhowl. "You can stop now. I'm not touching you anymore."

I snapped my mouth closed, ending my strangled-cat imitation. After a moment I muttered, "That was awful." I shoved my heels into the dirt to push myself back into a less uncomfortable position.

"Now I know exactly how to torment you." The delight in Lisa's voice was unmistakable.

"Let's get your mind off torture and get out of this piss pot. Where's the knife?"

"In my hand." She nudged it into my palm. "Just don't cut me. I'm not sure I have excess blood to lose."

I fumbled until I realized I wasn't going to be able to open it one-handed. Where was a switchblade when you needed one? "I need help," I said, and explained the problem. Between the two of us, we managed to pry the blade out.

Lisa held on to the handle and tried to reach my zipped wrist, but our tethered hands couldn't quite make it.

"You realize," she said after a couple of awkward attempts, "I can't see what I'm doing. I'm as likely to stab you as I am to cut the tie."

Pleasant thought. Not that she'd probably mind if I was out of the way, anyhow. Daddy-O wouldn't have to worry about me and could leave everything to his new golden girl. Bitter much, Shay? I ignored my own attitude and said, "Give me the knife and let me see if I can get to your tie. I'll go really slow, but if you feel something you shouldn't, yell."

"I certainly will."

"The good news, which I suppose could be bad news, is it's been a while since I sharpened the blade."

"Maybe stop trying to make me feel better and get on with it."

We managed to swap the knife. I leaned against Lisa for balance and tried to keep the back of my hand against her arm as I slid past her elbow and up toward her wrist. When my knuckles hit the edge of the tie, I stopped. "This angle blows."

When folded, the knife was the size of my palm. Extended, the entire length was just shy of six inches. I slid the handle into my palm and pinched the blade between thumb and middle finger so when it came time to saw I could press my pointer against the spine for pressure.

The edge of my thumb caught the zip tie. I slowly tried to wedge the tip of the knife between the plastic strip and the pipe.

Lisa squeaked. I stopped.

"You okay?"

"Yeah. Try aiming upward."

I retreated and changed the angle. "I think I'm good, but you holler."

Lisa's breath puffed warmly against my ear. "Just do it."

I wiggled the blade again. "You sure I'm not hitting anything vital?"

"Yes. Do it already."

I worked the blade back and forth, holding my breath as I waited for Lisa's scream. The seconds ticked by and she remained stiff but silent. I applied more pressure, mentally chanting, "Cut," over and over. Finally, the tie split with an audible pop, and Lisa's hand slipped from under mine.

Lisa shook against my shoulder and it took a second for me to realize she was laughing. "You did it, and I'm not even bleeding to death." She wrapped her now-free arm around me in an awkward hug.

For a minute or two neither of us moved. Finally Lisa leaned back. "Give me the knife." She bounded to her feet, her cuffed hand yanking mine sharply upward. I squawked.

"Oh, shit." She stooped fast. "Sorry about that."

My temper flared. "Just cut this goddamn thing off." The more stressed out I felt the harder it was to control my temper.

"Give me a second."

Something wet splatted my cheek. "Are you shaking your hand?"

"Yeah. It hurts like hell."

I figured the splats had to be drops of blood from the zip tie cutting into her wrist. Ugh. If we got out of here, we were going to look like we'd been on a killing spree.

The good news was the prospect of escape was looking up.

After much awkward sawing on Lisa's part, the tie securing my hand snapped. I couldn't begin to describe the joyous agony of blood recirculation. What a dichotomy. It hurt like a bitch, but the pain was infinitely welcome because it meant I was free—or, well, no longer attached to an immobile object.

Lisa pulled me to my feet, and blood began flowing south. After much foot stomping, the prickling sensations beneath my skin eased.

"I'm not cold anymore," Lisa said.

"Me neither. Now we need to get those doors open and beat it before they come back."

"I'm totally turned around. Where are the stairs?"

"This way." Without thinking I took a long step and was jerked by the remaining handcuff into Lisa like a yo-yo.

"Ow," she said.

"Sorry."

"How about we hold onto each other's hand and discuss things before we go anywhere?"

"Fine idea."

We stood in tandem, then did some practicing in the fine art of moving in sync. Reality was a little more difficult than picturing the actions in my mind. Once we were semifunctional, we got down to it. I was the pivot while Lisa circled around me, her arm stretched out, feeling for the wooden steps. Lessons in the blind leading the blind from the School of Hard Knocks.

"Aha." She reeled me in, and then I was standing next to her, my palm resting on one of the worn stair treads.

"How should we do this?" I asked.

"Good question. The doors open outward, so pulling the hinges is out."

"Let's see how much play we have to work with."

I remembered having to duck on the way down and reminded Lisa to watch her head. Feeling a little less like two clowns at the circus and more like stunt performers with *Cirque de Soleil*, we navigated the rickety stairs and stopped at the cellar doors, hunched over to keep from banging our heads. Gaps around the edges of the doors allowed narrow beams of moonlight in, and as she moved I was able to make out the planes and curves of Lisa's face. Her eyes were dark shadows, but even in the minimal light I could see the pinched look around her eyes. She was hurting at least as much as I was.

"Hear anything?" Lisa whispered.

I listened intently. All I could catch was sporadic bursts of wind, and maybe the howl of a coyote. "Nothing that sounds like the bad guys. What time is it anyway? It has to be close to sunrise."

"No idea. No cell, no time."

"Is there lip in that response?"

"Maybe."

"I guess as long as sarcasm still works, we're doing okay."

We braced our manacled hands on the uppermost step and pushed on one of the doors with our free hands. We managed to create about four inches of play. Through the gap I could see a bar of some kind wedged through the handles.

Cold tendrils breezed in through the cracks and I breathed the fresh air greedily. "What do you think's holding the doors shut? It's round. A mop handle? A branch, maybe?"

"Don't know."

It took a minute to coordinate our movements, and then as one we stuck our hands through the gap.

Lisa said, "I think I feel bark," at almost the same time I muttered, "It's a big branch."

"Maybe if we both push on the doors at the same time we can snap it in half," Lisa said.

"Worth a try."

We put our non-cuffed hands against splintery wood. I wished I had pen and paper to catalog slivers with my growing list of other injuries.

"Okay," Lisa said after rearranging her position. "Ready."

"Go!"

We pushed. We shoved. We heaved.

"Stop," Lisa called, and we slumped against the steps, breathing hard.

I tilted my head trying to stretch out cramped muscles. "This position is a neck killer. We need more leverage."

"Hmm." Lisa was quiet for a few long moments. "Legs."

"Legs?"

"Yes. Legs. I've moved some really heavy things by bracing my back against the wall and pushing with my legs."

"It's a great idea in theory, but there's no wall to use."

"I hate when you're right," she said, the mockery in her voice crystal clear.

"You do not."

"Do too."

"Do not."

"Fine. I don't." It sounded like she was smiling. "So what now?"

"Why are you asking me?"

"Because you're older."

"Pull the elder card, why don't you?"

"Own it."

"You are such a smartass."

Now we were both laughing. Laughing was so much better than crying.

I sobered and said, "Back to your legs."

"Oh, yes. Legs. How can we push those doors with our legs?"

"What if..." I paused as I tried to picture things. "This is going to sound crazy. Standing back to back with someone, have you ever linked arms and let them pull you over their back as they bent forward? We did it all the time as kids. Sometimes to pop kinks out, sometimes to just mess around."

"Kind of like an upside down aardvark?"

"That's funny. I think. Anyway, the kid is balanced, kind of flopping around, facing the sky, on the back of the person who's leaning forward."

"Guess I missed that as a kid."

"Let's make this a first then."

"And hopefully last."

"You don't know, you might like it."

"Maybe." Lisa sounded doubtful. "How do we do this?"

"Let's go back to level ground and practice. Come on." I grabbed Lisa's hand and slowly navigated down into hell.

Lisa abruptly sneezed twice, and then again.

"Don't wipe your snot on me."

"Wouldn't dream of it." She snorked hard and I grimaced, ready to yank my hand to safety in case she reflexively tried to wipe her nose.

For the next few minutes we took turns balancing each other on our backs. It actually felt pretty good to stretch my spine out after being bounced around and trussed up for so long.

"I get it now," Lisa said after she straightened and my feet hit the ground. "The question is how do we get into position up there?"

Good point. Whoever was on the bottom needed to support the other person's weight as well as try and stay balanced with one arm literally tied behind her. Plus, it'd take a lot of trust for whoever was on top to kick the doors. One wrong move by either of us and we'd both tumble down the steps.

I said, "Let's get as close to the door as we can but with room to maneuver. Whoever's lighter should be on top doing the kicking. I say we keep our uni-hand as neutral as possible so neither one of us is thrown off-balance."

"All right."

I detected hesitation in Lisa's tone but chose to ignore it. "Let's get this done."

We navigated upward again. The entire staircase shook with each step. I worried the entire thing would collapse from the pressure we were going to exert on it as we tried to leverage the doors open. But flaming out that way was infinitely better than sitting around waiting to be extinguished by two faux-leprechauns.

Lisa was big-boned, but I was denser and weighed more even though she was taller. Thus I was designated propper-upper and Lisa mad kicker. We sorted out who should do what and how. I braced my legs and leaned forward, keeping our conjoined hands steady by sticking my thumb through a belt loop.

Lisa rolled onto me, and we linked our free arms. Well, what a dumb idea. I couldn't hold us both up on a single riser without hanging onto something or else we were going to take a swan dive right into the Mold Void.

I explained the problem. We shifted again so I could settle the palm of my uncuffed hand against the super gross concrete edge of the foundation above. The girl better hurry because I didn't know how long I would last before my arm gave out. "Proceed."

"Roger that. Commencing Operation Bust Out." Then Lisa went after those doors with a vengeance. At first nothing happened.

"I think," Lisa wheezed, "I'm going to shatter the doors before I put a dent in whatever is holding them shut."

"Whatever. Just keep going."

After a flurry of vicious kicks Lisa yelped, "My foot went through!" She redoubled her efforts and I concentrated on keeping us both aloft. My arm shook from the strain.

"I think...I can slide...the branch out. I'm going to roll off. Hold on."

Once she disembarked I felt so light I could've floated right through the splintered doors. I straightened slowly, making sure not to lose my balance. Lisa stuck her head through the remnants of the door and wiggled the branch out of the handles. Then she pushed one of the cellar doors open. "Come on." She pulled me along as she scrambled out of the place nightmares lived.

I sucked in a gigantic lungful of unmusty oxygen. "Holy hell. We did it, Lisa."

"Did we...ever," she said, still trying to catch her breath. Her kicking portion of our escape had exerted way more energy than the propping portion, although the arm I used to hold us up still trembled.

My heart thundered as we tried to get our bearings. The moon was a sliver in a clear sky. Woods so thick they looked pitch black surrounded a house that wasn't much more than a dilapidated, two-story shack. Nearby was a smaller outbuilding that had mostly collapsed in on itself and a barn that leaned precariously to one side.

"Okay, sister," Lisa said. "What's our next—wait. What's that?"

The distant rumble of an engine sounded like it was coming closer fast.

We looked at each other and I whispered, "Run!"

CHAPTER FIVE

I had no idea how long we stumbled around trees, pushed through brambles and brush, and tripped over fallen logs in the blackness of the forest behind the haunted house. Nothing was an easy proposition in the dark, but add to it the fact we were literally hooked together, and it was a minor miracle we made it more than fifty feet.

At one point my foot caught a root. Suddenly I was airborne, pulling Lisa behind me. We tumbled down a hill into the muddy bed of a creek that, fortunately for us, was in dire need of water. Lisa was splayed across me. By the time she pulled me to my feet, the back of my head, my back, and the back of my legs were coated with thick mud that smelled of dead leaves and rot. Since I'd served as her landing pad, Lisa was spared the worst of it with the exception of her knees and the front of one leg.

I stripped most of the muck out of my hair. Lisa found a stick to squeegee me off, and then we were on the move again as the sky oh-so-slowly lightened.

I groaned. Every part of my body hurt. "How long have we been running?"

"Don't know. Twenty minutes? Half an hour? Why don't you wear a watch?"

"Hate that sweaty-under-the-band thing."

"No way."

"What?"

"That's why I don't wear one very often either."

The more time I spent with my long lost sister, the more I discovered we had in common. It was weird. Cautious optimism about the possibility of us getting along dared rear its head, and I surprised myself by welcoming the emotion instead of fighting it.

The darkness past the tips of leafless branches lessened, though not enough to make much of an impact on our ability to see clearly at ground level. Although the light of day would allow for easier going, it would also allow our captors to find our trail if they were looking. I wasn't a woodsy person but even I knew the path we'd left behind probably looked like it was made by a couple of rampaging moose.

A huge tree, bark pockmarked with age, had snapped near the base, probably during one of Minnesota's windstorms. Its upper branches were hopelessly tangled with that of its neighbors, and it hung suspended at a forty-five degree angle. At some point, I figured, those branches would give way and the whole thing would come crashing to the forest floor, begging the old "if a tree falls where no one hears it does it make a sound" question. It's funny, the thoughts that popped into my head during times of distress.

"Let's take a breather," I said and leaned against the trunk. Without much choice, Lisa settled beside me.

Every ache was beginning to make itself known. Now that the surge of adrenaline had faded and my heart slowed from about three hundred beats a minute to something a little less deadly, the early morning chill oozed down the nape of my muddy neck and I shivered. Exhaustion made my body feel as if it weighed ten times more than it really did.

"Cold?" Lisa asked.

"Yeah. And so damn tired. I'd have worn something warmer if I knew we were going to be rolling in the mud like a couple of piglets."

With her free hand, Lisa unwound the Harley scarf from her neck and draped it over my shoulders. "I think you need this more than I do. I'd loan you my jacket too, but this," she jingled our handcuffed wrists, "presents a removal problem."

"Thanks." I wrapped the scarf around my throat and buried my nose in the knit. It smelled like Lisa and like the Leprechaun and, surprisingly, made me feel better.

She gave me a whack. "We need to stay moving if we're going to keep you thawed out. I wish I hadn't left my gloves in your car." She flexed her hands a couple of times then stuck her unattached one in her pocket.

An idea came to me as I brushed my cheek against the scarf. "This thing is plenty long enough to cut in half. It'll still go around my neck and we can wrap the other half around our hands." I lifted my left hand and her right followed obediently.

"I like your thinking, O'Hanlon." I couldn't see her face well, but the smile was back in her voice.

I patted my pocket, and then felt the other. No telltale bladed bulges. "You have the knife?"

"No, I—" Lisa broke off to mirror my own self-pat down. "Shit. What did I do with it once I cut you free? Didn't I give it back to you?"

"Honestly, I have no idea. All I remember is trying to breathe and being terrified we were going to be eaten by a giant nightmare before the bad guys came back. Probably either left the knife in the cellar or lost it on the run. Maybe it fell out of a pocket when we tumbled into the mud." I released a grumpy sigh. "JT gave it to me as a Christmas present. Oh, well. Let's get moving."

As I straightened, the sound of not-distant-enough voices trickled through the trees. Every hair on my body sprang to attention. I clapped my hand over Lisa's mouth and whispered, "Listen."

She nodded and I released her.

We were too far away to clearly make out what was being said. The conversation sounded like at least two people, maybe more. Definitely male. What were the odds we'd run across some good old boys wandering the wilderness on an early Sunday morning stroll through the dark when it wasn't deer hunting season? Not good.

Lisa's lips brushed the shell of my ear. She whispered, "Stay or go?"

The decision was made when a beam of light flashed through the trees and painted the brush only a few feet from where we stood. If we made a break for it, we'd give our location away.

As if we'd been doing the tandem thing all our lives, we slipped as one around the fallen tree and crouched behind. Brush and brambles filled the gap between the angled trunk and the ground, giving us a modicum of concealment. The earthy scent of damp leaves was sharp this close to the ground.

Adrenaline flushed through my system again. I felt like a stock car, brake pedal pushed to the floorboard, engine screaming, tires spinning.

Twigs and leaves crunched as footsteps came closer.

I held my breath. Lisa entwined our fingers and held on tight. Time slowed, sound magnified. The treetops swayed in the breeze. I swear I could hear individual branches rustling.

"I don't know," a gravelly voice said from a couple dozen feet away. "We can't look for these bimbos all night."

Holy filet-o-fuck.

"Ain't night no more," another guy said. "It'll be light soon."

"We'll give it another half hour and then we gotta get to a phone so I can make the call. Both calls."

"But we don't have 'em."

"S'okay. Eddy doesn't have to know that. They're just a couple of girlies. They won't last long out here, and there's nowhere close they can run to."

I tensed, began to rise. Just girls, were we? I could show them a thing or two about girls.

"No," Lisa whispered in my ear. She let go of my hand and grabbed the top of my thigh, leaning her weight on it, forcing me to settle back onto my haunches.

Assholes. Now I wished this had been a Green Beans prank or someone's idea of a sick joke. Instead, there was no doubt in my mind these were the clowns who came to see Eddy yesterday morning. The Donald and The Nose. What were their real names? The Nose was the short one. Sheets, I think it was. Bobby was The Donald, tall and slick and conniving. A smarmy mouthpiece without substance.

What did they want with us? With Eddy? What had she said? That they thought she was in possession of something of theirs. What could Eddy have that was worth kidnapping us for?

A flashlight beam brushed our protective tree trunk, and swung away in an arc. I wasn't sure how close they were and tried to control my breathing.

Sheets said, "We promised Scooter we could make this happen, Bobby. We gotta deliver, or she's gonna send her two-wheeled team out for us. You know they don't miss."

Bobby said, "Don't worry, Sheets. We'll make this work. If Eddy doesn't come through, we'll find another way to put the squeeze on her. You know as well as I do she's the one who took it. The last twenty-five fuckin' years are on her. She owes us."

"We're a couple of idiots. Never should've made the deal with Scooter." Sheets sounded dangerously close to whining. "It should have been in our hands before we made this arrangement."

"Are you calling me a fuckin' idiot, Sheets?"

Uh-oh. This was turning into a weirdly disjointed, mesmerizing soap opera. What the freaking hell was the "it" they were talking about?

"No, Bobby, you're not an idiot. We just should've thought this through before making the deal with the jailhouse narc, that's all."

"How was I supposed to know he was hooked directly into crazy Scooter, the gigantic dickless dictator?"

What the hell did a gigantic dickless dictator have to do with Eddy?

Sheets mumbled, "I dunno. I don't want to be constantly looking over my shoulder every time I hear a moped."

"Hey. Don't you worry. I'm not going to see a year and a half's worth of planning go down the fuckin' toilet because Miss High and Mighty isn't coughing it up. We pull off this deal of a lifetime and it's easy fuckin' street after that."

A lot was apparently riding on this deal of theirs and for some reason Eddy was the key to making it work. That wasn't good. Not good at all.

"Come on, Sheets. Let's get moving."

"Wait a sec. I gotta take a leak."

"Christ fuckin' sake. There's a stump over there. Hurry up."

Uh-oh. Were they talking about our tree stump? Lisa's hand on my thigh squeezed harder.

Footsteps came close. I tensed at the scuffing as it stopped right in front of us. He was less than three feet away. My thighs began to burn from crouching. I desperately wanted to straighten my left leg before it cramped. But I knew one wrong move and we were done for. I put a hand on the tree for balance and prayed potty time would be over fast.

A zipper unzipped, followed by a splashing sound that went on and on. "Ahh," our tree pee-er said. He peed so long I wondered if he had an extra tank attached. "Better," he said as the tinkling slowed. A few more seconds passed and then the zipper zipped.

"Come on," Bobby shouted. "We don't got all day."

The duo noisily clomped off. Stealth wasn't a strong suit for either of them.

Once the sound of their movements faded, we cautiously stood. Good thing they left when they did because my legs weren't going to hold out much longer.

Lisa whispered, "Those two are mixed up in something big. What do they want with Eddy?"

I relayed their visit to the Rabbit Hole and ended with a truly sincere apology for accusing Lisa of being the cause of this kidnapping.

"You have no idea what they think Eddy has?" she asked.

"No. Eddy didn't say. I can't think of one thing she owns that someone would want this badly. Her television? Her collection of knitting and gambling magazines? I don't think she has much money in the bank."

"You said they were old. Like how old?"

"I don't know. Maybe sixty-five? Around Eddy's age, anyway." I frowned. "What if they go after Eddy?"

The thought stirred the Protector in me, and it felt good to let the heat of righteous fury spread through my veins. When I was a kid, Coop tagged me the Tenacious Protector because if a loved one was in danger, I could go from calm to terrifying in seconds. In those moments, I literally saw red. My last meltdown happened a few months back and involved a cop who was hunting my father. Thanks to JT's quick intervention, I hadn't landed head-first in the clink.

"The best thing we can do," Lisa said, "is get out of the big bad forest and make sure Eddy's okay." She glanced around. "Though I'm not sure which way to go."

"Not the way those guys went." I grabbed Lisa's wrist, and we quietly fled in the opposite direction.

Before we'd gotten very far, one of us stepped on a branch that snapped loud as a gunshot. We froze. Any way you looked at it, that loud crack was going to carry.

"Shit, shit, shit," Lisa muttered under her breath.

"Hey!" Bobby shouted. "What was that?"

Impossible to tell how far away they were.

Hand in hand, we bolted like bunnies running from a lawn mower. We zigged this way and zagged that. Dodged around underbrush, weaved through the trees like a couple of competing slalom skiers.

For long minutes we kept up a frantic pace. Finally Lisa yanked me to a stop. I couldn't hear sounds of pursuit, but we were panting too hard to make out much.

She asked between gasps, "Anything?"

"Don't think so." My heart was galloping as fast as the Clydesdales who thundered across the pasture to rescue their puppy from the big bad wolf in that Super Bowl commercial. They had some of the Protector in them too.

We set off again at a slower pace, listening for anything threatening, but that was hard to do when every sound freaked me the hell out. I refused to let myself panic at the thought of being lost in the forest wearing mud-covered clothes and a Harley scarf.

Eventually we ran across a narrow trail and with no better options we followed it.

After a while Lisa said, "How do you know we're not going in circles?"

"I don't. My idea of roughing it is a bed-and-breakfast without Internet. Maybe we should've followed that creek bed we fell into. Aren't there supposed to be settlements along rivers?"

"Maybe. But that didn't even qualify as a stream."

We hiked a while longer. The sky lightened to the extent we could actually see where we were going.

Lisa sighed noisily and finally uttered the dreaded words that I'd been trying hard not to think myself. "I have to go to the bathroom."

"How bad?" Using a privy at the Renaissance was one thing, but this was something else altogether.

"Bad. Had to go when you tried to drop me off at the apartment." She shifted in that way that said potty time better happen sooner rather than later.

"Pretty bad then, huh?"

She answered with a pitiful look of panicked desperation that would've been comical at any other time. "Why is it that when you finally decide you have to go, you *really* have to go?"

I rummaged through my pockets for something she could use and pulled out the wad of napkins I'd grabbed off a table at the Leprechaun.

Lisa peeled a couple off and handed me the rest. "For safekeeping. I'd hate to accidentally drop them…you know."

I stuck them back in my pocket. "How are we going to do this?"

To our right was a slight grade, and halfway up the hill lay a weathered, rotting log that had fallen sometime in the last century. I pointed at it. "How about using that? You can either hang your ass over it or squat behind it."

Lisa followed my outstretched finger and gave me a dubious look.

"What? You have a better idea?" I swept my noncuffed arm in an arc. "There's a distinct lack of bathrooms around here."

"I'm trying to learn not to hate when you're right."

"We're making progress then. Come on."

Brambles grabbed at my clothes as we plowed off the forest trail and plodded up the hill. Lisa mumbled, "I can't believe I'm going to do this."

"If you gotta go, you gotta go."

The fallen tree was about three feet in diameter, and at one point made a natural ledge if Lisa did want to air out her fanny. The log had been there a while—moss crept up one side. Bark was cracked and chunks lay on the ground around it. Most of its branches were either broken or eaten off, and one end of the trunk was collapsed.

"I can't do this in front of you," she grumbled as she unfastened her jeans. "I've got a shy bladder."

"For chrissakes. Then crawl over and I'll wait here."

Lisa scrambled over the log, and I perched on the rough bark facing away from her, extending my cuffed arm behind me. Suddenly, the arm was yanked backward. Before I could utter a peep, a hand was planted between my shoulders and stopped me from tipping head over teakettle.

"Sorry," Lisa said. "I don't have enough slack to get my pants down."

I rearranged myself and lay down on the log and closed my eyes, giving her more of my arm to work with. Moments later, Lisa groaned in relief. Finally she said, "Good thing I only had to pee." She wiggled around and I tried not to think about what was happening. "What should I do with the napkins?"

"What?" I asked as I idly pulled chunks of bark off the tree with my unchained hand.

"The napkins. I've heard you aren't supposed to litter in the forest."

"Are you kidding me? We're lost in the woods with some scary-as-shit men on our tail, and you're worried about littering?"

"Maybe."

I rolled my eyes. She really was too good to be true. "You want to carry them out of here with you?"

"Well, no."

"Well then?"

"Fine." My arm levitated as Lisa pulled her pants back up. "God that felt good. Sure you don't have to go?"

"I'm holding out for a real bathroom." I tossed a thick piece of bark away and sat up, facing Lisa as she struggled to work around my hand and button her pants. Her stomach rumbled.

"Man," I said, "you must be hungry."

"Hmm?" Lisa said, still fumbling with her button.

"Didn't your stomach just growl?"

"No."

Another growl emanated from right below my ass.

Lisa whispered, "That wasn't me."

The log shook as something inside it shifted. I yelped and shot to my feet.

"Something's in there!" I grabbed Lisa's cuffed hand with my own.

She bounced over the log, her momentum almost toppling me. I caught my balance and we bolted.

CHAPTER SIX

Eddy settled stiffly into her recliner. A cup of coffee in a mug on the side table and a warm cinnamon crescent roll on a plate in her lap remained untouched. She stared through the black screen on the television, trying to figure out how to proceed.

Just after JT had left the café to go to Lisa's place, the phone had rung. Bobby Temple, the ex-con who'd come calling the day before with his ex-con buddy Dwight Sheets, was on the other end. It'd been twenty-five years, and Eddy could easily go another twenty-five without seeing either of their ugly mugs again.

Eddy closed her eyes, the phone conversation churning in her mind like an electric beater folding brownie batter over and over again.

"Yo, Eddy. Baby."

"Who's this?"

"Eddy. I'm hurt. I just saw you yesterday."

"Bobby?"

"There you go. How ya doin', sweetheart?"

"I told you before, and I'll tell you again, you rat, I am not your sweetheart."

"Oh, I like 'em feisty. You raise 'em feisty, too, dontcha?"

"What are you talking about?" Dread bled through Eddy's veins with each beat of her heart.

"That girl in the picture. The one you're all cuddled up with. She means something to ya, doesn't she? And maybe that other babe too."

"My Shay? Other babe?" she echoed faintly.

"The one that looks like her but is fair-haired where *your* Shay," he sneered, "is dark."

"For the love of Peter, Paul and Mary, what have you done, Bobby?"

"Nothing much. Just provided a little incentive for you to return the five hundred Gs you owe me."

"I told you, I don't have the money. I never did have it. And how did you manage to steal that exact amount?"

"So it was in the ballpark of five hundred grand. We counted the bricks real quick in the car when we dropped Leroy at home before Sheets and me ditched the car. Whatever. And I'm not buying that denial, sweet cheeks."

"Bobby. You listen to me, you son of a ratfink. I do not have that goshdarned dough. Now you bring Shay and Lisa back here. This instant."

"I think you're lying, old lady. Leroy told us he was going to call you after the job. He was hot to tell you all about it. Sheets and I get there and what do we find? Leroy's dead carcass and all the money gone. What are we supposed to think?"

"I don't know what you should think, but you listen carefully, Bobby Temple. I do not have the money. Stop this craziness right now and bring those girls home."

"Can't do that, sweetheart. I need the money for…what shall we call it? A business transaction. It's a big one, baby. Great big."

"You're out of the clink for how long and you're back to the life already?"

"Prison never stops a businessman. Just hones the skills. So. The cash."

"I do not have five hundred thousand dollars. I barely have four thousand bucks in the bank."

"You're lying, Ms. Quartermaine. Tell you what. I'm a kind-hearted man. I'll give you till eleven tonight to give us a good faith payment. No payment, and your precious girls are gonna get hurt. Ten grand in cool cash keeps them in one piece. That'll give you a little extra time to do whatever you need to do."

Panic washed over her like a tidal wave but she said calmly, "I can't get into the bank until tomorrow. It's not open on Sundays, you nincompoop."

"Tomorrow then. I'm nothing if not a generous man. I'll give you till the end of the business day tomorrow. I'll call you later with directions, sweetheart. See ya soon."

Eddy jumped at the sound of the kitchen door banging open. She really needed to install a rubber bumper on the edge of that darn countertop. "JT?"

"Yeah, it's me," JT said. A metallic clang followed. "Your cake pan's on the counter. Looks like Shay and Lisa had a food fight in the street and then decided to sleep it off in Lisa's apartment. Little shits."

Eddy flinched as if she'd been struck with a cupcake herself. JT had about thirty seconds before her neatly organized world shattered like a mirror smashed into a million bits. "Grab yourself a drink and come sit down."

She closed her eyes and listened to bottles clang and the whoosh of the fridge door closing. Such simple, everyday noises. Comforting sounds taken for granted that were about to be decimated in the maelstrom she was about to unleash.

JT passed, her movement creating a breeze Eddy felt against her skin. She heard the heavy sigh JT released as she threw herself on the couch and the clang of a bottle cap against the glass top of the coffee table.

"What's the fire?" JT asked.

Eddy opened her eyes and set the plate holding her pastry next to her coffee on the side table. Time to pay the piper. She'd always known that one day the closet door hiding her skeletons might be opened, but never did she imagine it would be wrenched right off the hinges.

JT tipped back a long-neck bottle of root beer. Her throat flexed as she swallowed. Then she wiped her lips with the back of her hand and peered expectantly at Eddy.

Eddy said, "You might want something a whole lot stronger than that."

JT's eyes widened for a second and then narrowed.

Eddy pushed the recliner's leg-rest closed and sat forward, elbows on her knees. She could hardly believe she was about to spill her guts to a cop. But JT wasn't just any cop. She was family. But family who was still a cop.

"JT," she said, "I'm about to confess something to you I haven't ever told a living soul. Twenty-five years I've held onto a secret. I'm trusting you because there's no one else who's going to understand, and you're the only one who can help." Eddy released a resigned sigh. "Beyond that I'm ready to accept whatever comes my way." She risked a glance at JT, whose expression reflected confusion, maybe fear.

"What's going on?" JT said slowly. "Does this have something to do with Shay?"

"It has everything to do with her."

"But she's okay, with Lisa."

"Not exactly."

"What?"

"She's not exactly with Lisa. Well, she is with Lisa, but not at Lisa's apartment."

"What are you talking about? Where is she?"

"I'm not sure."

"What do you mean you're not sure?"

Eddy shrugged helplessly and JT's relaxed face morphed into a mask of panic. She said, "Is she okay?"

Eddy thought about the phone call. "Yes. She's fine. But you have to know this." She rubbed her hands together, threaded her fingers, and pressed her knuckles to her mouth. That's right, old woman, she chided herself. It's time to start praying. "I don't know where to…how to say this. Truly I never bargained for what I'm about to tell you."

"Maybe you should start at the beginning." JT's voice was flat, carefully modulated.

Eddy figured she used that tone to interrogate the bad guys. Even knowing JT as well as she did it made her squirm inside.

JT carefully set the root beer bottle on a coaster on the coffee table and focused on Eddy.

"All right." She tried to bring some order to her thoughts, which were spinning through her head like shiny steel shooters bouncing off the flippers of a pinball machine. "My husband—Clifton was his name—was killed trying to extricate his brother, Harley, from a nasty, nasty gang. They were a bunch of vicious, mean-hearted souls. Harley got caught up in the drugs, and when he started dealing, my Clifton did everything he could to get his brother out of the life. The night Clifton was killed, he'd found the house Harley was dealing out of. He was on the doorstep trying to convince Harley to come home when a rival gang drove by."

Eddy pursed her lips, eyes locked on the French doors across the room. "Clifton didn't have a chance." The shock of loss was as fresh and real as it was all those years ago. The ache she thought was finally gone hit like a physical blow. They, whoever they were, said you could run but you couldn't hide. They were right.

"Eddy, I'm so sorry." The compassion in JT's voice was overshadowed by obvious anxiety for Shay's welfare. The near-terrified expression on her face and the increased speed of her bouncing knee spoke volumes.

"Relax, JT. Everything's going to be okay." No other option was acceptable. But for "fine" to happen, she needed to finish this. "They dug thirty-four slugs out of that sorry excuse of a house. Do you know how many they dug out of my Clifton?"

JT didn't answer.

"Seven. He took two in the neck, one through his shoulder, three to the gut, and one straight through the back of his head. The cops said he was dead before he hit the ground. I want to believe that. I couldn't stand to think otherwise."

"What happened to Harley?"

"Little shit somehow escaped. Three months later he shot his sad self full of heroin. OD'd. He was a good kid, Harley was. I know he thought Clifton's death was his fault, and it was, along with a boatload of bad luck. That boy got mixed up with the wrong crowd and couldn't find the backbone to walk away. Of course, getting away from a gang like that outside a body bag isn't an easy thing to do. I know that."

"I do too, Eddy."

Eddy straightened, her hands gripping the arms of her chair so hard she saw her knobby knuckles go bloodless. She tried to relax, but was too upset. "I was pregnant with Neil when Clifton died. He wanted so badly to be a father. We'd been married for a couple of years at that point, trying for a child. Made it through two miscarriages. Found out I was pregnant the day—" Eddy paused and swallowed down the lump that rose in her throat "—the day he was killed. One of my biggest regrets was that I never had the chance to tell him he was going to be a daddy."

What she was about to reveal next to JT was something she'd never be able to shake until the undertakers shoveled dirt atop her casket.

"Eddy." JT made a move to rise, but Eddy waved her off.

In a thick voice she said, "Stay there or I'm not going to be able to finish the story." Eddy bounded out of her chair and disappeared into the kitchen. A few seconds later she was back with two tumblers and a half-full bottle of whiskey. She set the glasses on the table and splashed a liberal amount in each.

JT stared at her. "Isn't it a little early to be hitting the hard stuff?"

"Once I tell the rest, you'll be happy to have something to stiffen your spine. Cheers," Eddy said with zero humor. She handed a glass to JT and downed the contents of her own in one swallow.

The look on JT's face vacillated between bewilderment and guarded confusion. She sat frozen in place with the glass in her hand.

Eddy set her empty tumbler on the table. Her guts roiled as she again considered the ramifications of spilling her deepest secrets. Shay's best interests were the most important thing, and it was critical that she follow through, so she was going to lay it all out—damn the consequences. Best to do it as fast as she could before she lost her nerve.

"So Neil was born. I was a single mother, working as a head teller at a bank. That's where I met Linda, Shay's mom. That woman saved me. She became the best friend I ever had.

"Not long after Pete bought the Leprechaun, the house next door went up for rent. Linda talked me into moving from the north Minneapolis apartment where we'd been living. Shay was just a little squirt like Neil, and they got on like two peas.

"Linda babysat Neil if I needed a break, and I watched Shay when Linda needed a sitter. For a few years things were really good. Then Leroy came along."

Eddy grabbed the bottle and poured herself half the amount of her first dose, which she quickly dispatched. The burn at the back of her throat centered her. She cast another look at JT. The poor woman still hadn't moved. The liquid in the glass JT held rippled—her hand trembling. She'd picked up on the severity of the situation and was obviously waiting in dread for Eddy to finish. Son of a preacher man, this asinine mess was a terrible thing to lay on anyone. JT was an upstanding detective, and Eddy knew the gamble she was taking in airing the filthiest of her laundry to a police officer. But Shay was in trouble, and she was responsible, so she would do what she had to.

She took a breath and continued her story. "That jackass was trouble with a capital T. I have no idea what drew me to him in the first place. Old Leroy was a regular customer at the bank. Tall, dark and not so much handsome as charismatic. That man could talk a preacher out of his Bible. I fell for him like a bee drawn to honeysuckle. I had no idea the man fed off a terrible temper and had a really short fuse."

Unbidden memories washed over her, as intense as if they'd happened yesterday. Eddy bypassed the tumbler and grabbed the bottle, tipping it to her lips for a sip. The golden liquor burned its way down her throat and into her chest. She wondered how drunk she'd be at the end of this and didn't particularly care.

JT put her untouched alcohol on top of a magazine on the coffee table. "What happened?"

"At first Leroy was a real gentleman. Showered me with gifts. Took me out to nice places. Nicklows, the Bungalow. They're gone now, but back in the day? Mmm hmm.

"He was nice to Neil, too, at first. That son of a bitch weaseled his way into my heart like a tick burrows under the skin. The bastards drain you dry till you either rip 'em off or die trying." She laughed bitterly at the thought she was probably shocking poor JT with her uncharacteristic cussing. "Leroy was fickle. His personality turned on a dime. Everything would be fine, and the next second, fists were flying. 'Course I became his target."

Eddy met JT's well-on-the-way-to-horrified gaze. "He was abusive. A manipulator, just like all abusers are. I can see that now, but it took many years to understand how deeply his hooks pierced my hide.

"Anyway, I should've realized something was funny when he'd ask me 'bout the bank, innocent questions how this or that worked." Eddy shook her head, unmasked disgust marring her features.

"One night Leroy hoodwinked me into giving him an after-hours tour. I was terrified we'd get caught, but at that point I'd do anything to avoid him throwing a conniption. So I brought him in, showed him 'round. After that, he wheedled me into bringing him back a handful of times. It kept him happy, and a happy Leroy wasn't a belligerent, violent a-hole."

"Was he casing the bank?"

"What he was looking for was information, but not on the bank itself."

JT sat straighter.

"Do you remember hearing about the Eden Prairie Center armored car heist back in eighty-six? One of the drivers was murdered. The case was never solved."

"Sure. I was just a kid, but that robbery is legendary. Whoever pulled it off got away with a lot of money."

"That's right."

Rapidly changing emotions chased across JT's face until a look of comprehension settled on her features. "Leroy?"

"Yes, ma'am."

JT blinked, grabbed the tumbler of whiskey and tossed it back. She grimaced with a hiss and warily asked, "What does this have to do with Shay?"

Eddy splashed just a drop more into JT's glass. "That's where this gets dicey." She leveled her gaze at JT. "Keep your lips zipped till I'm through."

"Whatever you need."

Eddy set the bottle on the table beside her coffee. This was the point of no return. "Such a nice spring day. Wednesday, if I remember. Linda and I both worked early, were home by two, two thirty. We rode together because my car went kaput right after I moved into the rental, and Linda was nice enough to let me hitch with her. I was getting ready to whip up some brownies for the kids."

Eddy's lips twitched in a ghost of a smile. "Leroy called right around three. He was so excited I thought he was going to pee himself. And he was drunk. Skunk drunk. Believe you me, I'd seen him pickled plenty, but this time was different. Wanted me to come over, said he had something to show me. Something that was going to change our lives forever."

"Were you—"

"Shush, child." Eddy nailed JT with The Eye, and JT promptly clamped her lips together. "When he called, we'd been on the outs for some time. I'd not seen him for quite a while. A few months before, he hit Neil for spilling something, gave him a bloody lip. It was one thing to lay a hand on me, a grown woman. But—" Eddy wagged a finger, "—don't you touch my son. I went after him, but of course he got the upper hand and took me to town. Once again, I had to call Linda for help. She showed up at the ER, no questions asked. Gave me and Neil a ride home. That rat's ass had broke three of my ribs, blackened both eyes, bruised my kidneys and hit me so hard upside the head I couldn't hear right for a month. But from then on he steered clear of my boy."

Eddy took a sharp breath and picked up the bottle again, cradling it with both hands. "I'm ashamed to say that was the fourth or maybe the fifth time Linda had to bring me home from the hospital after Leroy worked me over."

"Jesus, Eddy—"

Eddy cut her off with one warning look. "Linda begged me to leave him. She was sure the next time he'd kill me. Was

our Eden Prairie Center branch because pine trees along the boulevard screened the building.

"They put that fake bomb on the hood of the armored car, just like the media reported. Threatened to set it off if the guards didn't open the truck. Those boys stuffed that duffel bag full of money. Somewhere along the line one of the guards made a move and those damn-fool robbers shot him dead. Leroy never told me if he did it or one of the other two scoundrels. No matter."

The enormity of what they'd done still stunned Eddy. Bad enough to think about what happened all those years ago and entirely another thing to give voice to it. It was like having the worst out-of-body experience ever. "What they did was no different than if he'd killed my boss and shystered the money right from my own bank's vault."

JT blinked fast, as if the movement would help process the words she'd just heard. Eddy grabbed the whiskey bottle and dashed a titch more into JT's tumbler. "Down the hatch."

JT obeyed. She scrunched up her face and wheezed, spinning her hand in the universal "carry on" motion.

"I was fit to be tied. How dare he do something like this and drag me into it! We were all going to wind up as lifers, and I had a child to worry about.

"Couldn't decide between giving that ding-a-ling a piece of my mind or hoofing it out of there but I felt like my feet were glued to that filthy floor. I was appalled. Absolutely livid. Told that stinker in no uncertain terms I thought he was a thieving, murderous ass.

"Oh boy, JT. The look on that man's face. He couldn't believe I wasn't over the moon about his big news. Dumb fool. One thing led to another and my bad attitude about his new fortune set him off on a wild rage."

JT made a sound somewhere between a growl and a moan.

"Told me if I didn't want to be a part of his new life, there was no reason for my own to go on." Eddy put a hand to the back of her neck and tried to squeeze the tension out.

"By the second punch, I knew Leroy meant business. He was going to kill me. Sure as the sun rises and sets." Visceral images, sounds of that violent afternoon echoed through her mind, and she fought to keep herself from breaking apart. "He held me against the couch, a hand around my throat, the other whaling on me.

"Couldn't breathe. Somehow, got my legs up between us and shoved him hard as I could. Leroy tripped over the coffee table. Down he went." She squeezed her eyes shut. "Back of his skull bounced off the fireplace hearth. Son of a bitch was stunned. Was going to run, but he came back 'round, got to his knees and calmly said, 'I'm going to kill you now.' Looked like he had the devil in him. I grabbed that shotgun."

Eddy squared her shoulders and met JT's wide-eyed gaze. "And pulled both triggers."

CHAPTER SEVEN

The forest had lightened up considerably while we walked. A ways back we'd come across a more substantial path that intersected the twisty deer trail. After a brief discussion that almost escalated into an argument about which way to go, we'd let the toss of a coin settle the direction, and off we went. Boy, we were both headstrong and stubborn.

The newscasters were wrong about snow in their forecast. The sky was bright blue, and if I wasn't covered in mud I might've been able to appreciate the rugged beauty of our surroundings. White-yellow rays of sunlight splashed through the trees and dappled the brown leaves covering the ground. Exhaled breath still fogged the air so I guessed the temp was probably in the upper forties. I hunched my shoulders, burrowing my face into the scarf around my neck more for comfort than warmth.

I shot a glance at Lisa. Her face was mud-smudged, hands reddened from the cold. Below the cuff of her leather jacket, her nonmanacled wrist had dripped blood from where the zip tie had cut into it. Rivulets that'd run down the back of her hand had dried a stark, rusty maroon against her skin. Mud flaked off the knees of her jeans.

The back of my pants stiffened as the mud fell off and they began to dry. The material on one leg had a six-inch gash where I'd caught it scrambling through the splintered door of our prison, and my hands and forearms were scraped up and mud-streaked. We looked like a couple of escapees from the prison bus that'd rolled down an embankment onto the train tracks in the movie *The Fugitive*. Yeah, we were fugitives, all right. Fugitives from the bad guys.

The path widened, and we were able to walk abreast. The footpath meandered along a running stream that grew in size and volume the farther we traveled.

Periodically one of us called a stop, and we'd listen for signs of pursuit. In those moments I held my breath, waiting for the leprechauns to come crashing through the bush. Thankfully, we hadn't heard anything except noise of our own making and the harmonies of Mother Nature.

Our trek into the unknown allowed me time to chew on our predicament. Why would Bobby and his shorty sidekick care enough to get physical? I wracked my brain for what Eddy might have that they wanted so badly. Her truck was an old crapper. I didn't think she had any jewelry worth anything. Yeah, she owned the Victorian that housed the Rabbit Hole and her apartment, but what could they do with that?

The trail curved to the left, up an incline, and then down again before flattening out. Walking in tandem was sure easier on a level surface.

Lisa cast me a sideways glance. "What are you thinking about so hard that your eyebrows are almost fused together?"

I walked her through my thoughts. "I can't think of anything Eddy has that those two numbskulls would want bad enough to do something like this. It's crazy." I kicked at a broken branch.

"I guess we won't know till we get back and Eddy tells us."

If we live that long, I thought.

A few minutes later, Lisa asked, "What was it like? Growing up with your dad?"

"What do you mean?"

"Obviously you guys didn't always see eye to eye."

I laughed. "We still don't. It's gotten better, though."

"Did you always have problems?"

Did we? "Not before my mom died, I guess. I remember everything being good then."

"What happened to your mom?"

I swallowed and let my gaze hop from maple to pine to oak. If this were a different place and time, I probably would've told her it wasn't any of her business. But I could feel things between us shifting. Maybe a little soul sharing would do us both good.

"When I was seven, there was an awful car crash, a terrible accident."

"And?"

I shrugged, fixed my gaze on the path ahead. I could simply not answer, and leave Lisa with the bare bones of the most traumatic event in my life. Or I could open up and let her in more than I ever had before. As much as I didn't want to admit it, Lisa existed because of my father's weakness at a time when his need was greatest. She was blood. And to me, blood always meant loyalty. Would that change if I shared this new truth?

Lisa was part of my family whether I liked it or not. The facts weren't going to change, and it might be easier if she knew exactly where I'd come from. I shook the sleeve of my hoodie over my hand to warm it and gripped the cloth in my fist. "We were in the car and someone hit us. My mom died instantly. Eddy's son, Neil, was killed too. Eddy pulled me away from the wreck."

The handcuff jingled as Lisa's cold fingers found mine. She gave me a reassuring squeeze. We walked in silence for a couple of minutes. Lisa didn't push for more, apparently willing to wait me out.

The words weren't so bad to say as long as I didn't think too much about them. "Eddy held my intestines in with her bare hands while we waited for help. She saved my life."

Lisa squeezed my hand again. "Jesus. I can't imagine surviving that, what you went through."

"After that, my dad—our dad," I acknowledged, "had his hands full trying to raise me and run the bar. As far back as I can remember he loved his hooch, and he loved it even more after the accident." I blew a heavy breath. "Living next to the bar meant Eddy mostly took over raising me. She was always there, chauffeuring me to sports stuff, to all the things kids get involved in. She'd often try to get Dad to come along. Once in a while he did, usually to my track meets. More often he stayed home with his bottle. Like I told you before, when I came out in college, he flipped the fuck out. Seriously. Up until JT arrived on the scene we were barely civil to each other. Any communication we had was all surface." I laughed bitterly. "Man. There's no doubt where my temper—and yours—comes from."

"But after JT things got better?"

"It was rough at first." I veered around a tree stump, pulling Lisa after me. "Once he got to know her, saw us together, I think he realized how good she is for me. She calms my soul in a way no one else can. It's only been about a year that he and I have really gotten along, been able to relate on any kind of deeper level."

"I had no idea. I'm sorry, Shay. Now I totally see how his accepting me was so hard for you to take. I never meant to get in the way or come between the two of you."

"I know. I'm sorry too. Really. I'm a hardheaded shit sometimes."

"Thanks for telling me. I know it wasn't easy."

"It's probably a good thing." I gave her a wry grin. "Confession is good for the soul, they say. Let's get ourselves out of here in one piece and start this," I waved my hand between us, "over."

"Clean slates are becoming my forte." Then Lisa laughed, the sound more a snort than anything else. "If we don't wind up finding our way out of here, I wonder if anyone will stumble across our skeletons. The handcuffs would link us together for all eternity." Lisa gazed into the distance, a contemplative expression in her eyes. "I wonder if we'd still be attached at the wrist in heaven."

I prodded Lisa's ribs through the leather of her jacket. "I—" The words caught in my throat as we rounded a bend. Maybe a quarter mile distant was a break in the forest. The leaf-strewn trail we'd been following widened into a chalky-colored path lined on both sides by dead grass. Beyond that a rust-colored cupola topped a silver metal roof attached to a white structure. I couldn't see more than the top third of the building for the trees blocking my view. "Look!"

It took a second for Lisa to register what I was pointing at. Once she zeroed in on it, she gave a whoop and charged ahead, dragging me along until I sorted out my feet. Then I was flying alongside my sister, our arms pumping in sync, making a beeline toward what I hoped like hell was safety.

CHAPTER EIGHT

Eddy studied JT's pale face with a critical eye. "You need another dose? Medicinal purposes only, of course."

JT held out her glass. Eddy delivered just enough for one swallow and replaced the bottle on the side table.

The amber liquid in the bottom of the tumbler must have been mesmerizing, because all JT seemed to be able to do was stare at it.

"Drink up, sister." Eddy needed JT on her A-game, not so stunned she couldn't speak.

JT hesitated then did as she was bid. After a moment, she give Eddy a leery look. "Jesus. Who'd have guessed?" She tucked her hair behind an ear and shook her head once, as if she'd been punched herself. "Okay. Go on."

Eddy rested her fists on her thighs, nails digging into her palms. It didn't take much to fall back into that horrific moment, although over the years she'd honed the ability to compartmentalize with the best of them. But when that door to the past was cracked open, the tang of gunpowder overwhelmed her senses and she could feel the cold, hard weight of that cannon in her hands. She tasted metallic blood, hers and Leroy's both, in the back of her throat.

She was back there in that terrible place, with its stained hardwood and old house stench. Staring in horror at the hole in Leroy's chest and the growing puddle of blood that blossomed from beneath him like a moss rose opening in the morning sun. The shotgun had slipped through numb fingers and clattered against the floor. Voices in her head had howled so loudly she couldn't think.

Eddy blinked herself back into the present. Tried to focus on JT. "When that gun went off, the kick knocked me smack-dab onto my keister. I was so beat up I had a hell of a time getting back to my feet. When I finally did I saw that Leroy wasn't breathing. Didn't even twitch. For just a blessed second I was safe. Neil was safe."

Eddy felt her eyes glaze. "But I shot a man dead."

"Listen to me." JT bridged the space between them and grabbed her hands. "You acted in self-defense. It's justifiable homicide."

"Not in those days. Not for somebody like me. Probably true these days too, for African-American women." Eddy squeezed JT's fingers and let go.

JT released an audible sigh. "I know. Go on."

"Where was I? Was about to skedaddle, that's where. Saw that damn bag of money. Don't know what got into me, but I scooped it up, scrammed out to the car and drove home."

JT slopped some liquor in Eddy's glass and held it out.

This was turning into one hell of a day. Eddy accepted the offering. The alcohol burned its way into her system. She felt like she was watching herself through an ever-changing kaleidoscope—detached, frenzied, and whirling. "I made it home. Tried to clean up. Then I hauled my caboose up to Linda's apartment above the bar like the devil himself was breathing hellfire.

"Poor Linda. The look on that girl's face when she saw me. She hauled me into the bathroom before the kids got a gander at the damage. Refugee from a biker bar fight was what I looked like. She doctored me up, and while she did that I told her what happened.

"JT, Linda was a rock. Didn't even blink. Just asked how she could help." A sudden lump corked off Eddy's words. Losing control was out of the question. She had to finish what she started. For Shay. For Lisa. And maybe, if they all survived this, for herself.

"Between Linda and me, we decided it was high time Neil and I visited my sister in Mississippi. Linda agreed to let me know when things cooled down and we could come home. She helped me pack, then we rounded the kids up and headed for the bus depot."

Eddy could see the tension in the stiff way JT was holding herself. She asked, "What happened to the cash?"

"Don't know why I took that damn blood money in the first place. I stowed that bag in the oven and left it behind."

JT caught Eddy's eyes. "Hey. We're going to work this out. You were the victim here. What happened next?"

"Linda mashed the pedal to the floorboard. We knew we had to make tracks because Leroy's despicable friends could be on the way to his place at any time. We hit a stoplight." Eddy squeezed her eyes shut. "The light changed. Would've made it, too, but a big old truck ran the red, plowed into the intersection and creamed us." She opened her eyes and met JT's. "I'm the reason Shay's mother and my Neil are dead."

CHAPTER NINE

We cleared the wood line and thundered toward a rudimentary road that intersected our path. After a few hundred feet, a white picket fence ran along our left side in front of a grove of trees, and to the right, beyond a patch of brown grass maybe fifty feet wide was a churning river. I wondered if it was the same one I'd taken the header into, although this tributary contained a whole lot more water than my muddy creek bed.

Another hundred feet and the trees on the left parted to reveal a cream-colored two-story house with maroon trim. On the side of the building facing our path, banded maroon and cream pillars held up a three-foot by five-foot overhang and a door was nestled in a fully enclosed porch. Three windows to the left of the door were placed in a diagonal line rising toward the roof, with the third, topmost window on what was probably the second floor. A fourth window was parallel with the third, directly above the porch. The pattern was odd, like an upside down hockey stick.

Lisa whooped. She veered toward the fence and then pulled up short. I stopped just short of colliding into her.

She smacked the fence. "Where's the damn gate?"

The fence extended to a ninety-degree angle and disappeared around the corner of the house. Maybe there was a gate on the other side.

"Boost me over," she said, giving my cuffed wrist a yank.

"Ow! Hey, easy." I hoped for a miracle because I was going to need one to survive this without something becoming dislocated.

"Sorry. Got excited."

If that kind of headstrong action was what my friends and family had dealt with all these years—and I was pretty sure that was the case—I owed them a gigantic debt of gratitude and perhaps a few apologies. Maybe a deeper understanding of self might rub off the longer I hung around my sister. Surprisingly, I didn't think that prospect was necessarily a bad thing.

A couple of attempts later I managed to boost Lisa over the fence. After a bit of fumbling and some creative profanity I cleared the boards myself and we were standing in front of the maroon and cream screen door. Drapes covered the porch windows and did a good job of keeping prying eyes out.

Lisa glanced at me. "You gonna knock?"

"You were the one who was all hot to hop the fence and get over here. Don't let me undercut your glory."

She raised a fist and paused. "What if the bad guys are inside?"

"We won't know if we don't knock."

"Don't you think we should at least have a plan if it is them?"

"How about if the bad guys open the door we run like hell."

"You're just full of bright ideas, aren't you?"

"What do you want from me?"

"Apparently nothing."

I shifted to face Lisa with narrowed eyes. "Nothing, huh? Is that so?"

Lisa leaned into me, eyes equally narrowed, shoulders hunched. I did the same thing when I was on the brink of an altercation. "Yeah, that's so."

I clapped my free hand over my mouth and stepped back. "What are we doing?"

She blinked a couple times and straightened, her shoulders dropping along with the constipated look on her face. I hoped I didn't look like that when I was all wound up but figured I probably did.

"Sorry," Lisa muttered. "It's like watching myself in the mirror." With that she turned and gave the screen door three sharp raps.

We waited what felt like an hour but was probably no more than thirty seconds, poised to make a mad dash away. Lisa looked at me, lifted a shoulder. I stepped forward and delivered a few whaps. Still no answer.

I pulled her down the two steps to the ground and around the corner of the building. This side apparently constituted what would be considered the front. An awning over a veranda ran the length of the structure and was held up by four banded pillars matching those on the side of the house. A six-foot log had been cut in half lengthwise and provided a natural step up onto maroon-painted slats. We hopped the log in tandem.

Two windows on either side of the door were similarly cloaked in white drapery, effectively obscuring any interior view. Whoever lived out here embraced privacy in a big way. I pounded on the "screen" door. The screen had been removed and replaced with a pane of glass, probably to keep out the cold.

We knocked for a good five minutes.

"Come on," Lisa muttered and gave the wood on the side of the door a healthy punch.

Yup, she was a chip off the old ice block all right. I grabbed her hand again before she could vent a second time and towed her across the yard. Beside the house, a two-story brick building was sandwiched between it and another redbrick building that extended in an L shape out to what I could now see was an unpaved road. The fence ended against the side of that building. A stone walkway bisected the grassy expanse and led from a gate in the fence to a door in the center building that was framed by two windows. Here again our knocks went unanswered.

We retreated to the gate. It opened easily—the latch wasn't stiff or rusty. Whoever lived here kept things in good working order.

An uncovered twenty-five foot plank deck fronted the third building. Two wood-shuttered windows and a door painted the same cream and maroon color scheme as the wood-clad house faced the street. In fact, all of the windowsills and doors on the brick structures matched.

I said, "What is this place and where is everyone?"

"Maybe it's the kind of town where everybody goes missing because the inhabitants are used for sacrifices. Then there's a huge cover-up and anyone who comes looking disappears too."

"Where do you come up with this stuff?" I pegged her with a dismayed glare. "You sound like a conspiracy theorist. Or you've been reading one too many Gerri Hill books."

Lisa gave me a blank look. "Gerri Hill?"

"Don't you read lesfic?"

"What the hell is that?" The stubborn, stony tone Lisa fell into when I was getting on her last nerve was alive and well. I'm ashamed to admit the contrary part of me clapped its hands in delight.

"You're a bad lesbian. Lesfic. Lesbian fiction. If you'd read *Keepers of the Cave* you'd know what I was talking about."

"Hey, come on. I'm going to college. College students never have time to read for fun."

We traipsed onto the deck, past the shuttered windows. I banged hard on that door for a while. "Three for three? Really?"

While I'd been thumping away, Lisa worked to pry one of the shutters loose. I gave up knocking and stepped closer to allow her a wider range of motion.

"Aha!" Lisa tugged at the wood and swung the shutter open, revealing the glass beneath. We both pressed into the space, jostling for position. I cupped my hands around my eyes to block out the glare.

A long, dark-stained wooden counter ran maybe halfway down one side of the space. On top of the counter were a couple chalkboard slates and scattered pieces of chalk, some well-used textbooks and a contraption holding a big roll of brown paper. A bit farther down, a wood-framed glass case probably held jewelry or some other expensive items. Or maybe that was where they displayed the fudge. Not that I saw any indication of fudge, but my stomach growled and I was on the verge of hangry—an excellent word that was a delightful mash-up of hungry and angry.

Behind the counter were rows of shelves holding bottles and containers of various sizes, books, boxes of dry goods, and other assorted items.

"Looks like a general store to me. And where there's a general store there's food," I said gleefully, elbow deep in visions of fudgy goodness.

"You think this is an Amish settlement or something?"

"Dunno. And come on. Don't tell me you're not hungry. If you're related to me you're starving."

Lisa didn't answer. Whatever. I caught sight of a waist-high wood barrel next to the counter lined with cloth and filled with familiar shapes. I poked Lisa squarely in the side. "Check it out, in that barrel there. Is that what I think it is?"

"Ow! Stop that. Where?"

"There."

Lisa followed my finger. "Oh yeah. Peanuts. In the shell."

"We need to get in there. I'm fucking starving."

She gave me an incredulous look. "And how do you propose we do that?"

"Break in."

"Are you shitting me? Break in? I'm a lot of things but a thief's not one of them."

"Come on, Miss High-and-Mighty. Desperate times. We have to eat something to keep up our strength. God knows when whoever lives here is going to come back. Maybe they're in cahoots with the leprechauns. We don't even know where the freaking hell we are, and we probably shouldn't stick around too long."

"I still hate when you're right. How much money do you have?"

"What?" This woman was a whole different brand of weird. Where'd that question even come from?

"If we break in to take some of those peanuts, we're going to leave money to fix whatever we wreck."

Wow. The girl had a serious conscience. But she was right. I probably would have come up with the same thing if I'd been thinking with my brain and not my belly. "Deal."

I pulled everything I could find out of my pocket, and Lisa did the same. Between the two of us we put together almost two hundred bucks. The tips had been pretty good last night.

We spent at least five minutes trying to figure out the easiest way to get inside and settled on the tried-and-true smash-a-window method. Another few minutes and Lisa scrambled gingerly over the windowsill behind me, taking care not to slice up her hooha.

The first thing I noticed was the smell. Stale and musty. Somewhat reminiscent of the cellar we'd run from but not that pungent. But, if "ancient" had a scent, this was it. The second thing I noticed was a light layer of dust on everything. No one had been in here in a while. Maybe the town's populace really did get sucked into a black hole.

Lisa dusted her hands off as best she could. "Holy stinkballs, I can hardly breathe."

"Let's get the booty and vamoose before we get busted with our mitts in the goobers." I tugged Lisa to the barrel of peanuts and shoved a handful into my pocket. She laid the agreed-upon hundred bucks on the counter and dug into the barrel herself.

My mouth watered in anticipation, and I couldn't wait a second longer. I cracked one of the shells open and popped two perfectly shaped nuts into my mouth. I bit down and instead of a satisfying crunch, I felt one of my molars shift. "Ahhgah!" I spat the remnants of peanut into my hand.

"What's wrong?"

"These are harder than a damn diamond. And they taste like shit."

We both gazed down at the conglomeration of spit and nuts in my palm. I ran my tongue around my teeth, thankful none of my back molars was missing a chunk.

"Not edible," Lisa said.

"No."

Lisa handed me a wadded napkin.

I held it up between two fingers and surveyed it suspiciously. "This isn't from earlier is it?"

"Well, yeah."

"That's disgusting." I dropped the napkin. "Why did you keep it? Are you crazy?"

Lisa looked blankly at me for a moment and then her eyes lit up. "You think I used it and hung on to it? You really think I'd stick a dirty toilet paper napkin in my pocket?"

"You're the one who asked what to do with them." I bent over and snatched it from the floor. "How was I supposed to know?"

Lisa rolled her eyes and I wiped my hand.

Now that my feeding frenzy had come to an abrupt halt, I stowed the napkin and took a better look around. A big glass jar labeled FLOUR was half-filled with white powder. Another contained what looked like crunched-up leaves and was tagged TOBACCO. The label on a corked, green-tinted bottle read TINCTURE OF ABSINTHE and next to that sat a container labeled DR. KING'S NEW LIFE PILLS.

Hanging off one of the shelves behind the counter was a yellowed sign fastened to a piece of cardboard. Two wire ties secured a rudimentary clay pipe to it. I leaned closer for a better look. For the exorbitant price of five cents, you could be the proud owner of a kid's toy bubble maker. Near the bottom of the sign was a date.

"Oh, for cripesake."

"What?"

"Look." I pointed at the sign. "1905. We're in a goddamn museum in the middle of bumfuck Minnesota. At least I think we're still in Minnesota. Hell. We could be in the middle of bumfuck Wisconsin for all I know."

"Those peanuts are probably antique too. They're so old they're petrified. Ha!" Lisa pointed at me. "You ate a petrified peanut."

"Tried to eat a petrified peanut." I let out a disgusted breath. "That would be why it's so musty in here. Crap. Let's get moving before we get busted for raiding the antique parlor."

"Wait. Maybe there's something in here we can use to try to cut the chain between the handcuffs."

"Good idea."

For five minutes we hunted for some kind of implement to handle the task. A pair of ancient garden shears didn't even dent the metal. A rusted, five-foot, two-person saw gave me some hope but after a number of awkward attempts and nearly severing my wrist, we wisely gave up that idea.

I left the money tucked under one of the chalkboards and we vacated the mercantile, making sure to secure the shutter across the broken window. Then we checked the barn and the other outbuildings, but the place remained eerily uninhabited.

After a debate on which direction to take, the toss of a quarter guided us to the right. We trudged down the white gravel road away from the ghost town. That made me think of Dorothy and the Yellow Brick Road. We'd just been to Oz without the Wizard, and we needed to get back to Kansas before the Wicked Witches of Leprechaun Land hunted down our sorry asses and turned us into munchkins.

CHAPTER TEN

"I'm the reason Shay's mother and my Neil are dead."

JT rocked back on her heels. Yeah, baby, the hits just kept right on coming.

Eddy stared tensely at JT, guilt and regret reflected in her eyes. "Don't go gawping like a goshdarn fish, JT. Say something."

JT snapped her mouth shut. As a homicide investigator, she'd seen the worst of the worst. She'd been witness to the horrific damage one person could inflict upon another. She understood some motivations and others not at all.

But, in doing her job, she could at the very least try to find justice for the victims, attempt to bring some kind of peace to them and the loved ones left behind, and that's what kept her going. It's what drove her.

Within that framework, a fine line existed. She'd witnessed victims who'd become aggressors—those who, when pushed far enough, fought back. And she got that. Occasionally the letter of the law overrode the spirit of the law and the victims who saved themselves wound up behind bars, because, after all, taking a life was taking a life, wasn't it?

Not in her world. Sometimes taking a life was the only way to stop someone from killing you. She didn't need a jury to tell her that's exactly what happened in Eddy's case. Everything revolved around the circumstances of the event, and these circumstances indicated an act of nothing more than self-preservation. She'd seen it too many times. The abused would not leave the abuser, and sooner or later the violence escalated to the point of no return.

As these thoughts whipped through her mind, her swirling emotions settled. She met apprehensive black eyes with her own. "Listen to me." She squeezed Eddy's arm. "It's okay. You acted in self-defense. You're safe. Do you understand me? Your secret is safe."

Eddy's lips trembled and she pressed them together.

"Breathe."

Eddy complied.

JT said, "Linda cared about you and was happy to do whatever she could to help. You can't blame yourself for the accident."

"I can and I will until my last breath escapes this beat-up old body. It's just the way of it." Eddy shuddered, and then shook like a wet dog. "Okay. I'm back in the game. Sit your tush down. Still got more confessions."

JT eased back to the couch and gritted her teeth. What more could there be?

"I gotta make it make sense for you."

"But—"

Eddy held up a hand. "Not a word. Please. Just listen."

JT slapped a hand over her mouth.

"Good girl. Now, back to the worst day of my life. Bobby and Sheets were coming by Leroy's later that night to split up the money. When they got there, they found a dead Leroy and no money. Now keep in mind these two yahoos are a couple of bumblers. Always were, still are. Remember that as I tell you this."

JT hesitantly nodded.

"The police got a call about a fire at Leroy's place. The house went up like tinder, burned hot and fast. Right to the ground.

Those nincompoops, Bobby and Sheets, were caught lurking a few doors down, watching. Neighbor called them in. Both those doofuses had gasoline on their hands, on their clothes. On their shoes. Idiots. Then the cops found three gas cans in Bobby's car and that pretty much sealed the deal.

"Not much left, I guess. They did find Leroy." Eddy's expression took on a look of wonderment. "The prosecutor went after Bobby and Sheets for manslaughter and arson. They wound up taking a plea deal, don't remember exactly what now. I was off the hook, and those no-good nitwits got what they deserved, 'specially since one of those poor armored car drivers was murdered."

"What did you do with the money?"

"Honestly, I forgot about it for a time. My little boy was gone. Linda was gone. My mind was gone. Pete was drinking like a fish. I couldn't eat. Couldn't sleep. Was a wreck. Without Shay, without her needing a mama to help her through her grief, I don't know if I could've kept going. Seems like weeks passed before I snapped out of it. One night I was going to heat up some fish sticks and tater tots for supper. Poor kid had been surviving on peanut butter and jam and takeout that Pete ordered. I turned on the oven, and before it even preheated, there was a terrible smell and smoke leaked out the oven door. I opened it and there was that dirty, greasy duffel bag. I pulled it out, doused the smoldering bits. Realized I could be in big trouble. If I gave the money to the police, they might think I was part of the robbery. I decided to hide it and think about it somewhere down the line when my mind was clearer. All I knew for sure was that I couldn't tell a soul, and decided I'd never spend it. Not ever."

JT's mind whirled. Holy shit, the secrets this little old lady kept. Straight out of an episode of the *Twilight Zone*. She pressed the heels of her hands to her eyes and felt herself freefalling into a big fat void. "Is that it?"

"'Fraid not. Yesterday afternoon, Bobby and Sheets showed up at the Rabbit Hole. Nearly lost my dentures when I saw who Shay called me out to talk to."

"You have dentures?"

Eddy rolled her eyes. "No. Turn of phrase."

JT clenched her teeth again in an attempt to forestall other observations. She was buckled onto the crazy train headed directly for the loony bin.

"Anyway, those boys are out of the clink and they think I have their money. They want it back."

"Why do they think you have it?"

"When they went to Leroy's place and found him dead, the money gone, they figured one of two people could've snatched it. Either Leroy's coke dealer—he owed a boatload of dough to the man—or me. They knew Leroy couldn't wait to tell me all the ways our lives were going to change. Boy did our lives ever change." Eddy paused long enough to tip the bottle back for another snoot and held it out to JT.

JT held a hand up. "I'm good." She wasn't drunk, but she could feel the alcohol in her veins. Any more and she'd cross the line.

"So when they showed up yesterday, I brought Bobby and Sheets back here for a chat. I tell you, I'd imagined that moment every time I couldn't sleep. I've prayed for a quarter century it would never happen. They told me they knew I was the one who'd taken the money because Leroy's dealer told them Leroy never paid off his debt. Couldn't believe that dealer's still alive, but that's neither here nor there.

"'Course I denied I took the dough, insisted I didn't have it, but they didn't buy it. While they were in the kitchen, Sheets picked up one of the pictures I keep on the sideboard of Shay and me, and then Shay herself charged in like a bull when things got a little heated."

"How did you explain to her what was going on?" When Shay was in protective mode, trying to divert her attention was like trying to wrestle a rare steak from Bogey the bloodhound.

"Told her everything was fine, and to get on out of here, then ignored her. Felt bad about that but it couldn't be helped. Was a good thing she was trying to finish up work before the festivities at the Leprechaun, and that kept her occupied." Eddy sat back in her chair, and for the first time, JT could see how worn out she looked.

"I didn't think much of the visit, figured them boys would leave it be. I should've known better."

JT could feel the buildup in the air, as if vibrating molecules multiplied a thousandfold.

"Early this morning I got a phone call. Bobby. Told me he and Sheets have Shay and Lisa."

JT inhaled sharply, and Eddy cut her off before she had a chance to get wound up. "If I give them the money they'll return the girls."

"What did you tell him?"

"Told him I didn't have the money."

"But you do. Jesus Christ, Eddy." What was she thinking?

The woman before her looked more miserable than ever. She didn't even get after JT for taking the Lord's name in vain. "No, I don't. If I did I'd give it to them in a minute."

JT abruptly stood and said in an uncharacteristically high pitch, "But I thought you didn't spend it."

"I didn't. Then Pete started getting Shay's doctor bills— that poor girl needed to have three surgeries before they were done patching her up. And then there were the bills for Linda's funeral. The casket, the burial vault, the plot at the cemetery. The funeral itself. Pete had no money for any of it. I kept fronting him what he needed. Linda's life—her death, I mean— was my fault."

JT's thoughts ping-ponged between how much she could withdraw in cash advances on her ATM and credit cards and rounding up her police buddies and pulling out the stops on a full-out search-and-rescue mission. Where in the hell did she and Shay stow the personal identification numbers for advances on their credit cards? She was pretty sure they'd kept them somewhere safe. In the safe maybe. And her partner Tyrell, the one person she could trust to keep his mouth shut, was sitting on that goddamn stakeout so he wasn't going to be able to help. Plenty of cop pals owed her favors—

"JT!" Eddy said sharply.

"What?" JT smacked a hand to her thundering heart.

"Pay attention. Sit your butt down. We have to think through this strategically."

"But—"

"I know Shay is in danger. But with those two it's really not danger-danger. I know you feel like you need to do something right this moment."

Holy shit, the woman could be infuriating. "But someone—"

"Let me finish explaining, and then we can make a plan. These two dimwits are nothing but conniving numbskulls."

"One of them murdered that guard, Eddy!" JT spit the words out so fast it sounded like her mouth had turned into a machine gun. Her eyes were wide and her body was vibrating.

"Easy now. I understand. But at heart, they really are a couple of bumblers. We can out-think 'em once you get the rest of this story. And it needs to be told. Now." Eddy stared pointedly at her.

JT perched on the edge of the couch cushion, every muscle tense. She forced herself to focus on Eddy and not let panic overtake her. "Okay. Go."

"Back to the money. Shay needed help with college because Pete wasn't able to save any money for her education. The bar itself needed a few cash infusions. Eventually I bought this place." Eddy swept a hand through the air. "After a while I felt less and less guilty about spending that cash because for the most part I only used it to make life easier for two people I cared most about in this world. I'd hurt them. Their lives were the worse for knowing me. I realize the accident was completely unintentional but nonetheless, me and my problems were responsible."

Behind the visceral fear she felt about Shay and Lisa in the hands of a couple ex-cons, JT felt the pain behind Eddy's words, and felt terrible for everyone involved. Shay, who'd lost a mother. Eddy, who'd lost a son. And Pete, who'd lost a wife, and come very close to losing Shay. "So how much do you have left?"

"I just used the last of it to pay for the renovations at the Leprechaun. There's not a dime left, JT."

"Nothing?"

"Zilch."

"What did you tell them?"

"That I didn't have their money and no way could I get my hands on half a million dollars. They didn't believe me. Bobby told me I have until eleven tonight to get ten grand together, and the rest of the money by tomorrow evening. He's supposed to call and give me directions before the meet-up. If I don't hand over the dough he says they're going to hurt the girls. I don't really think he'd do anything, but he is desperate and desperate people do dumb things. We just need to figure a way to get the girls back, then deal with Ding and Ling."

JT's brain exploded. She now understood what "blowing your mind" felt like, and it wasn't pleasant. At all.

Eddy jumped up from the chair and grabbed JT by the shoulders. "You listen to me, JT. Bobby's a dope, but he was never violent. Neither is Sheets. He's really a big old puppy who follows Bobby. Neither of them are like Leroy."

The only predictable thing was that nothing about this situation was predictable. Knowing Shay, it hadn't been a peaceful capture. What was happening to her? To Lisa? Were they hurt? Anger bled into fear and it seeped into her chest, but she swallowed it down to simmer uneasily in her gut.

Think. She needed to think. One step at a time. "So they want ten thousand dollars by tonight. We come up with that and it buys us a little time."

"Yes."

"Do you have any liquid assets?"

"I got four thousand I can pull from the bank, but not till tomorrow. There's fifteen hundred or so squirreled away here at the house."

"We've got a little bit in savings, and credit cards. I wonder what's in the Rabbit Hole account."

Eddy scrunched her nose. "I'd like to keep this away from Shay's business, but if we have to, we have to. That would mean bringing Kate in, and I'd rather not. She's got her hands full already."

JT and Eddy spent the next few minutes brainstorming cash acquisition strategies. The sound of footsteps thundering down the staircase between the Rabbit Hole and Eddy's place interrupted them. Rocky and Tulip charged into Eddy's living room.

"JT Bordeaux and Miss Eddy!" Rocky's voice was tight with excitement. "Tulip overheard you talking about money. Specifically that you needed to raise ten thousand dollars to get our Shay O'Hanlon and Miss Lisa Vecoli out of the clutches of some very bad someones." He gazed adoringly at Tulip.

Maybe their special abilities included psychic powers too.

Tulip said, "I'm sorry for eavesdropping, but I couldn't help hearing your conversation when I came down to get some hot chocolate from the Rabbit Hole. That hot chocolate is really top-notch." She smiled brightly for a moment, and then her face fell. "Shay is in trouble and needs our help." She gazed affectionately at Rocky and then turned to Eddy. "We have eight hundred ninety-four dollars and six cents from our savings account piggy bank to add to the Save Shay and Lisa Fund. We have to leave exactly fifty dollars in the pig, though, because that's how much Eddy gave us to start our savings account in the first place."

A lump lodged itself in JT's throat. Here were two of the dearest human beings she'd ever met, and to whom much of the world turned a blind eye because they were "different." Even with hardly anything to their name, Rocky and Tulip were willing to wipe out their savings to help someone they cared about. That was loyalty and love.

CHAPTER ELEVEN

A phone call from Detective Tyrell Johnson, JT's partner, broke things up. The cop who'd relieved JT had come down with his kid's stomach flu and had gone home puking out his car window.

The task force lead, Special Agent Dean Malachuk, had ordered Tyrell to call JT and tell her to get her ass back ASAP. Malachuk himself was on his way to help hold down the fort until JT arrived. This was his first time leading a multi-jurisdictional task force, and his already high-strung nature was shifting from frenetic to crazed micromanager the closer they got to go-time.

No way could she explain to him why she couldn't be there without exposing Eddy's secrets and endangering Lisa and Shay. That meant she had to show up. Goddamn rocks and hard places. If all went well, Malachuk would take off when she got there, she could explain the situation to Tyrell, and get back on track.

JT felt like barfing out her own car window. Air. Lots of air. In through the nose and out the mouth. Her head was spinning, her face was numb. Maybe she was having a stroke. Regardless of Eddy's reassurances, the thought that Shay was in danger nearly drove her insane.

Top that off with Eddy's revelations, and she had no point of reference for anything. Never would she suspect the woman to have it in her to blow someone away. Never would she have guessed that Eddy—tough cookie that she was—would've put up with one second of abuse, let alone repeated beatings. At least she'd bailed when the bastard laid a hand on Neil.

She refused to even consider turning Eddy in. What happened twenty-five-plus years earlier was a clear-cut case of self-defense. That bastard got what was coming to him, although the law might not agree only because, like Nixon, the cover-up had become the crime.

But the money... The robbery money was another big, fat wad of fucked up. How could she say a word when the woman had used the dirty dough for Shay's medical expenses? If Eddy hadn't, Shay may not have survived. JT's guts clenched at the thought. She couldn't fathom it.

Pete had needed funds for Linda's funeral, and he'd struggled with Leprechaun expenses over the years. So Eddy had spent her self-described blood money in whatever ways she thought might help.

That thought led to another. Had Pete ever wondered where Eddy's cash came from? Not that it necessarily mattered. Maybe he never knew her well enough to understand where her money originated. JT knew Eddy had picked up a job at some point in social services, again probably to try to help those who couldn't help themselves. Giving what she could to those in need was certainly a theme that ran deep.

JT wheeled around a slow-moving car and passed a bronze-colored Randy's Environmental Services garbage truck as she peeled off I-94 onto highway 252 toward the city of Anoka. The only thing she knew about the burg was its self-proclaimed status as the Halloween Capitol of the World. Too bad right now the tricks were overriding the treats.

She tried to focus on anything but Shay, on what might be happening to her. JT impatiently tapped her thumbs against the wheel. Highway 252 was a pain in the ass. Three miles, six stoplights and too many brake lights during rush hour. The stretch could easily take twenty minutes to navigate if the lights didn't cooperate. This time, however, she made it through without touching her brakes.

Stoplights navigated, JT's mind inevitably went back to chewing on the problems at hand. What a cluster. An armored car robbery, dead people, heisted money, ex-cons, a kidnapping? It sounded like a bad made-for-TV movie. The one solid thing she could concentrate on was the money. Money would buy them time to figure out how to take these two guys out and retrieve Shay and Lisa. Between Eddy's forty-five hundred bucks and Tulip and Rocky's donation of almost nine hundred dollars, they were still over five grand short.

Her own financial obligations and Shay's rather meager income from the Rabbit Hole didn't allow for much extra in the Bordeaux-O'Hanlon coffers. She did have a portion of her paycheck funneled into a pension account through the city, but no way she could access that in time.

Wait a minute. What was wrong with her? Coop. Good grief. Sometimes the simplest answers were so close you looked right over them. There was a very good chance Coop might have a stash of greenbacks. Since he'd been working his IT jobs, his financial situation had drastically improved. And he was kind of a cheapskate who usually erred on the side of hoarding his money rather than blowing it.

Okay. She felt a little lighter. She pulled her phone out and dialed his number. It went through to voice mail so she said she needed him to call back as soon as he had a chance. Then she rang Eddy to tell her to check in with Coop, but she didn't answer and JT left another message.

Now she could concentrate on the next item on her Get-Everyone-Out-Of-This-Stupid-Mess agenda. As soon as she could escape the stakeout, she needed to run checks on Bobby Temple and Dwight Sheets and find out what addresses were linked to them. It was likely Lisa and Shay were being held somewhere that was familiar to one of the two men.

She took a good look at the clock on the dash. Goddamn Malachuk. They had less than twelve hours to get shit together and the seconds were ticking by like lightning.

Fifteen minutes later she pulled into a thicket of brush on a side road and parked. It was a five-minute hike through the woods to the surveillance location, a ramshackle tree house/ hunting shack constructed a long time ago in a huge old elm about twenty feet above the forest floor. The structure had been found during a sweep of the area in the early stages of the operation. The focus of the investigation was a farm about a quarter mile distant. In the summer, leaf-cover blocked any view of the house, but in winter, with a little help from some surreptitious lopping of pertinent branches, the sightline worked nicely.

Based on what was panning out to be good intel, the two-and-a-half-story farmhouse was a drug storage facility for one of the Mexican cartels running meth up the Interstate 35 corridor. A bust of the magnitude they expected was the kind of thing that, if the winds blew the right way, could make a career.

Right now she didn't really give two shits about making her career. She just needed to get through the next little while until Malachuk satisfied himself that things were running smoothly. The closer the task force was to moving on the house, the more unpredictable the man became. Night before last he'd wanted to come out and observe during JT and Tyrell's shift, but there was hardly room for two people inside the hunting shack, much less three. They'd successfully talked him out of it. She thought a few Xanax would do him wonders.

Once Malachuk took off, she'd fill Tyrell in. She knew he'd be willing do whatever he could to help.

The sun cast broken shadows through leafless branches swaying in the breeze, and the brown remnants of summer's growth crunched beneath JT's boots as she followed a barely discernable trail. She shuddered under her jacket, which had been issued to her by one of the DEA guys. The M65 military parka was a couple sizes too large with a zip lining that usually kept her plenty warm enough. Now, however, her shivering was nearly uncontrollable.

As she closed in on the shack, the usual earthy smell of the forest was cut by a familiar, gut-churning scent, sharp and repelling. JT wrinkled her nose and put a hand over her face. Ten feet from the base of the surveillance tree was a pile of something that looked suspiciously like last night's dinner. She cautiously skirted it. Hopefully no one else on her team had come down with the stomach flu.

She gave a quick, low whistle and two seconds later a rope ladder was dropped from what looked like a very small house in a tree. Another few seconds and she'd scampered up and reeled it in behind her.

The shack was approximately five feet by seven. Rough-hewn logs split in half made up the floor and the walls, and white-rusted corrugated tin was pinned to the roof on top of more halved logs. Foot-high windows were cut out of three sides. A plank attached to the base of the windows gave hunters a place to steady their rifles. At one time this would have been a top-of-the-line deer stand. Now two camp chairs occupied the space, and an old bench served as a containment area for surveillance stuff including binoculars, audio equipment and a battery-run monitor with views that cycled through three cameras hidden in the house under observation.

Tyrell's long frame was scrunched into the camp chair furthest from the door. He was similarly dressed in a worn flak jacket, black jeans and scuffed tactical boots. The cord of a white earbud hung from one ear, the color vivid against his dark skin. Midnight-black eyes were glued to the video feed.

Malachuk was in the other chair, out of place in a knee-length overcoat and suit pants. His usually well-gelled blond hair was a mess, and black smudges stained the hollows under his eyes. Even if he was a pain, she knew he was under a hell of a lot of pressure.

"Bordeaux," Malachuk said. His voice was thick with exhaustion. "You're not feeling sick are you?"

She ducked to keep from hitting her head on the low ceiling. She was feeling ill, but not for the reason he expected. "Not at all. How are you, Tyrell?"

"Just fine," he rumbled without taking his eyes off the tiny screen.

JT gave Malachuk a bright smile. "We're good here."

Malachuk stared at her for a moment as if trying to assess the veracity of her words. Then he lurched out of the chair and promptly bashed his head on a crossbeam. "Goddamn," he muttered, rubbing the top of his head. "Let me know if you need anything or have any more...problems."

"You got it, boss," Tyrell said.

JT tossed the ladder and Malachuk descended. He lifted his hand in a brief wave then disappeared down the trail. JT stowed the ladder again.

"Hey," he said without looking up. "Sorry to call you back so soon."

When JT didn't answer, he shifted his eyes from the screen and squinted at her. Ty knew her almost as well as he knew his own wife, and his ability to sense when something was wrong was uncanny. Trust between the two of them ran deep and true. From the moment they met in the academy they'd always had each other's backs. And always would.

Tyrell's deep voice registered an octave lower when he asked, "What's going on?"

JT collapsed into the chair beside him and wondered where to start. In the end she related the pertinent facts of what had gone down since she'd crawled into bed this morning and found it empty. She skipped the part where Eddy blew away a madman, deciding she didn't need to burden Ty with that kind of moral dilemma. He'd lay his life on the line for her, as she would for him, but he didn't need to carry the added guilt of knowing something like that.

By the time she finished, Tyrell was leaning forward, elbows on his knees. The relaxed, focused person he'd been when she first arrived was gone, replaced with intense, agitated cop. Exactly how JT felt.

"Jesus Christ."

"I know."

Tyrell rubbed his eyes. "You have to go. I understand, JT. I get it. I'll be fine here till relief shows. Malachuk will never know." He nudged her leg with his boot. "Go to the precinct, see what you can dig up on these scumbags."

"You sure there's no one else we can call in?"

"Nah. I'll be good. Just keep me updated. If I can do anything let me know. Nothing's supposed to go down yet and we'll get notice when it does. Get outta here."

"Ty, I—"

He waved her off. "Just get your girl back. Oh, hey. You have a backup battery on you? Mine's dead."

JT dug out a black, playing card-sized USB power pack from a jacket pocket and handed it over. A dead phone in the middle of nowhere was never a good idea. "Three charges left on it so it should hold you for hours."

"Thanks. Now scoot and don't step in the puke on the way out." Tyrell pulled out a portable Igloo cooler from under the bench and cracked it open. "Snack for the road?"

The cooler was loaded with cold cuts, cheese, a box of crackers, two apples, a banana, some cashews, a handful of Hershey's Kisses and a neon Post-It with a hand-drawn heart.

"If the rest of the crew only knew what a big teddy bear you really are, you'd never live it down."

"I'm not a teddy bear. I'm a grizzly. Now scat."

She did. Ty stuck his head out the door as he pulled the ladder back up. "Watch yourself, JT."

She gave him a thumbs-up as she backtracked, navigated around the puke and faded into the trees.

CHAPTER TWELVE

By the time JT arrived at the precinct, it was noon. She made a beeline for her desk in the squad room.

The radiators were still radiating plenty of heat even though the temps outside had mellowed. The old building was often too hot or too cold, but for once she welcomed the almost oppressive warmth.

Eight sets of two desks were arranged throughout the squad room. The walls were painted Carolina blue, thanks to a past police chief who believed the shade induced better concentration. That outcome was still up in the air.

An office belonging to the lieutenant faced the bull pen. Every time JT saw his two windows blanked out by white slat blinds, she was reminded of zombie eyes. Another office had been converted into a war room, complete with a not too beat-up conference table, some ragtag chairs and three whiteboards. The last office had become a half-assed break room.

JT shrugged out of her jacket and slung it over the back of her chair. She kept her head down, hoping anyone who saw her come in would think she was too busy to bullshit. She impatiently tapped a pen against the keyboard as she waited for the machine to boot.

The room buzzed with the usual air of caged anticipation and the business of fighting crime. Five detectives were in, busy working on various tasks. Two talked to a woman in cuffs wearing a tight miniskirt. Mascara streaked her cheeks from a recent bout of tears.

The light in the LT's office was off, and if JT was lucky she could run her checks and get out before he returned and questioned what the hell she was doing. Since she'd been loaned to the task force, she swung by to catch up on administrative details every couple of weeks. Her appearance now wouldn't seem so out of place if she hadn't been in four days ago.

Finally the black screen popped to life, displaying the MPD log-in. It took three fumbling tries before she managed to type in the correct password. She was about to enter Dwight Sheets into the system when Detective Tom Shaw, unrelated to the Tommy Shaw of Styx fame, exited the break room with a steaming cup of coffee. Unlike the diminutive singer, this Shaw was well over six feet, and probably tipped the scales at two-fifty. The only resemblance came from the gray-blond goatee they both favored. "Hey Bordeaux, you're back."

Damn it. Shaw was a great detective and a nice guy, but he had a propensity for nosiness, which was probably why he was so good at his job.

"Just swung by to grab some records, then I have to beat it."

"I'm outta here." He saluted her with a raised mug and, thankfully, walked out.

"See ya, man," JT muttered under her breath. Her back was so stiff she felt like her shoulder blades might burst through her skin. She returned her attention to the monitor, finished inputting the name. No one else better come along who wanted to chat or she might accidentally punch them.

Twenty minutes later, armed with hastily put together files for both Dwight Sheets and Bobby Temple, JT made her escape unscathed. Safe in the car, she thought about contacting the probation officers of both men, but quickly discarded that idea because they'd obviously want to know where she'd gotten her information. The two men's residential program status info and temporary transitional housing addresses were in the files, but those locations would be the last places they'd drag two kidnapped women. She knew about channels she could go through to pull land ownership records, but time was too short to go for them, not to mention the fact that an inquiry would leave a trail.

She pulled out her cell and called Coop.

"'Lo?"

"Wake up, sleepyhead. I take it you haven't checked your messages."

"Uh, no."

"We have a situation."

* * *

Coop lived on Garfield not far from Lisa's place. Less than fifteen minutes after calling him, JT pulled to the curb in front of his place. Another two minutes and she was sitting on Coop's well-worn living room couch waiting for him to pull his hung-over ass together.

It felt good to be in this familiar place, with its scent of old socks and french fries. And pizza. A grease-stained pizza box sat on the coffee table. JT lifted the lid. Two slices of cheese pizza—testament to Coop's vegetarian ways—with what looked like triple the mozzarella lay congealed inside, along with a pickled pepper. Her stomach growled.

She inspected the goods first from one angle and then another. Looked mold free. She glanced at the top of the delivery box. A white sticker displayed Coop's name and yesterday's date. That should be safe enough. She grabbed both pieces, folded them together and went to town.

The quiet buzz of electronics bled from the dining room into the living room, and the steady hum helped her relax as she chewed her way through her impromptu lunch.

The dining room, which was a dining room in name only—was a long and narrow space loaded with hard drives, monitors and lots of interesting gadgets. Coop was an unreformed hacker and did contract computer work from home. His abilities seemed to only grow sharper as time passed. If anyone could dig up something useful on the bozos holding Shay and Lisa, Coop would be the one.

He was a gamer, sometimes losing days online playing MMORPGs. She wasn't sure what that stood for, so she thought of it as MORE PIGS PLAYING GAMES. She wasn't sure if that was a subconscious reflection on what she felt about her profession. On occasion Coop threw gaming parties that were nothing short of legendary. Once in a while, she and Shay had joined in on the fun, allowing their imaginations some free rein. It was probably good for her sanity, JT reflected, considering what she saw and dealt with on a daily basis. Too damn bad she couldn't lose herself in an online game right now.

She stuffed the last of the crust into her mouth and was chewing it when Coop clattered down the stairs and entered the room wearing blue jeans and a Green Beans for Peace and Preservation sweatshirt. She had to give him credit. His complexion was remarkably non-green the day after a holiday celebrating the Emerald Isle.

"Sorry," she mumbled through a mouthful. "I was suddenly starving."

"No problem." Coop disappeared into the kitchen. "Want something to wash that down?"

"Please."

Thirty seconds later Coop bounced onto the cushion beside her with a banana in his armpit, a bottle of Coke in one hand and a can of Mountain Dew in the other. He handed her the Coke, cracked the tab on the Dew and sat back, tilting the can high. She watched his Adam's apple bob as he swallowed. And swallowed.

"Ahh." He swiped a forearm across his mouth and crushed the can between his hands. "That's better." He executed a perfect free throw into a box next to the front door that was already half-filled with similarly squashed aluminum blobs. Next, he removed the banana from under his arm. He tossed the deep yellow peel on top of the pizza box and wolfed the banana down in two bites. "Okay. What's up?" He muffled a long belch behind a hand.

"Breakfast of champions."

"You know it."

"I need you to plug a couple of names into your magic system and see what you can dig up as far as addresses or land they're connected to, specifically where someone could be held without raising any red flags."

Coop gave JT a speculative look. "This have something to do with the call about Shay earlier?"

"You still didn't listen to your messages, did you?"

He shook his head.

Time was ticking and every second exploded like fireworks in her brain. But he needed to know what was going on. She gave him a super succinct sixty-second version. Before she finished, Coop assured her he could get hold of enough money to cover the ten thousand dollars and was already working his multiscreen computer, searching for places either Sheets or Bobby Temple might logically hold Shay and Lisa.

Coop squinted at the monitor, JT crouched beside him anxiously watching. She said, "You're sure this will stop when it hits on something?"

"Yup. When it finds the parameters I loaded, we're in. Patience, my fine five-oh. Why don't you go get us something more to drink?" Coop glanced pointedly at her.

Taking the hint, she abandoned her position and headed for the refrigerator. Surprisingly, the kitchen was devoid of takeout refuse, and the dishes in the sink were clean. She checked the forty-year-old Admiral fridge, and pulled out another can of Mountain Dew for Coop and one for herself. Might as well mix caffeine sources. Maybe it would help her brain function.

Coop popped the top and only drank half this time.

"For a vegetarian," JT said, "you're not too strict about what else goes in your body."

"Do what I gotta do. You should know how that goes."

"True. Cheers."

They clinked cans and Coop refocused on his search. JT wandered around his workspace. She picked up an object that looked like an egg, then bobbled it before she caught it. Coop's head whipped around as if he'd been slapped. "Hey! Take it easy with that."

"What?"

"My friend Adam is working on something that—oh never mind. Just set it down. Gently."

She shot him a sharp glance but did as she was told. "Is this something I should arrest you for?"

Coop's eyes narrowed. "It's best not to ask too many questions. You want my help or not?"

"Sheesh. Okay, okay." She stepped away from the intriguing curiosities covering the table. "Are we there yet?"

* * *

Armed with a very short list of addresses linked to the two ex-cons, JT and Coop set out in search of the shanghaied sisters. Dwight Sheets's cousin's house was in Eagan, a suburb southeast of St. Paul. The house was located in the type of community where, if anyone did any screaming, someone was sure to hear. JT ranked it low on the Places to Stash Shay and Lisa list.

They checked out Bobby Temple's sister's place in the Fridley Terrace mobile home park. Sis hadn't seen hide nor hair of her loser brother in the last twenty-five years and she wasn't going to start caring about his whereabouts now.

They thanked the woman for her time and returned to the car. JT found her way out of the park, and a quarter mile down the road pulled into the parking lot of Biff's Sports Bar & Grill. Really? Biff's? If any name belonged near a trailer park, Biff's was it.

She killed the engine and rubbed her temples. She was a cop, for fuck's sake. Why couldn't she shake the fog of terror and think straight? She needed to pull her head out of her ass and get in the goddamn game. "This is taking too much time. In that list of addresses you have, which location would be the optimum place to hold two hostages? Somewhere away from things, clear of nosy neighbors."

Coop scanned the sheet he'd printed out. Then he pulled his phone out and fiddled with it for a few seconds. "Okay. A relative of Bobby Temple's owns some land down in the southeastern part of the state. It's, like, a couple hours away. Would they have driven for hours with two pissed-as-hell chicks in tow?"

JT gave him a grim smile. "Is it rural?"

"Has a fire road number. It's in the southeastern quadrant of Minnesota, closest sizeable town is Preston. Population thirteen hundred. Yeah, I'd say that's rural."

"How far away from Preston?"

Coop tapped on his cell some more. "Twenty-three miles. There's one other burg, Carimona, population two hundred seventy-two, about halfway between Preston and Temple's address. Or let me rephrase. Temple's grandmother's place." He thumbed the keyboard. "We can make it down there in…about two hours and thirty minutes. Unless you ride the cherries and berries and haul some serious ass."

"Can do." She could get them down there in less than two hours if she pulled out all the stops. "Let's go."

Coop rubbed his hands together. "I always wanted to ride in the front seat of a cruiser at high speed instead of in the back headed to jail."

"You've been in the front seat all day."

"Not at ninety miles an hour, I haven't."

"And what makes you think I'm going to do ninety?" she asked, screeching out of Biff's parking lot.

"Because Shay is involved. Of course you're going to do ninety. Maybe a hundred." Coop sounded dangerously gleeful.

CHAPTER THIRTEEN

The road Lisa and I meandered alternated between bleak forest and brown field, up gently rolling hills and down the same. Not one car passed. Nor did we see any sign of human habitation.

My throat was so dry it crackled when I swallowed, and my unattached wrist was stiff and crusty with dried blood. The good news was the walking kept us both warm, and some of my aches diminished with movement. Speaking of movement, I was going to need to have one sometime in the near future. The faint gurgling in my guts moved from hunger to a more insistent and persistent pain. I ignored it and concentrated on the sound of the off-white gravel crunching beneath my feet.

Small talk and speculation about why this was happening had petered out a few thousand steps ago. Lisa marched resolutely beside me, beset with the same problems but not complaining. She really was a decent human being. And I was coming closer to accepting it.

We cruised down a forested hill and around a curve at the bottom. A half-mile farther, the road abruptly ended in a T.

Straight ahead, a cut-cornstalk stubbled field stretched as far as I could see. Pale pebbles covered the crossroad, and the view was identical in either direction. Trees, fields and grassland—maybe pasture. Rinse and repeat.

"Which way?" Lisa asked.

I shrugged. "Maybe we should cross the cornless desert. There's got to be a farmhouse somewhere."

Lisa's upper lip twitched at the suggestion. "*Children of the Corn*. Saw that movie, and now cornfields freak me out. I don't even like corn on the cob."

"Good to know for our annual Fourth of July blowout. I'll eat your portion. Anyway, the corn's all cut down. You can see everything. There's not a kid in sight."

She huffed. "Okay. It's a change of scenery. Sort of."

A ditch ran between the road and the field. We hopped it and struck out across the cornrows.

After a bit Lisa said, "Hey, is that a mirage or a grove of trees over on the right?"

I squinted. There did appear to be a dark blob off in the distance. Often in corn country the immediate area around a farm was a grassy, tree-filled oasis in the middle of an ocean of soil. "I'm channeling your vision. Let's go."

Estimating distances proved deceptive. After fifteen minutes of slogging along furrows and over stalky stumps, the blob finally morphed into trees. A house, a barn and three silos nestled behind the line of trees. Another five minutes and two cars parked in front of the house came into view. By this point I had to go to the bathroom so bad I could hardly stand up straight.

"Come on!" I grabbed Lisa's hand and increased the pace. Finally we crossed the tree break into the yard.

The sprawling farmhouse was white. The barn and silos were cobalt blue. The well-kept condition of the place gave me a surge of confidence, followed by an even more urgent urge to find restroom facilities, posthaste.

We leaped the three steps onto a covered porch and pounded on the front door. Likely rescue and the prospect of a real toilet combined to weaken my knees with sweet relief.

Until a bloodcurdling scream from within rent the air.

My arm froze midpound and I glanced at Lisa. Her eyes were as wide as mine had to be. I took a step backward as another shriek shook the foundation. Then a woman shouted, "Stop it! Stop it! Oh my freaking God, this really hurts!"

Holy shit. The Protector within me reared and took a good long sniff. If one of my loved ones was screaming their fool head off, I wouldn't have hesitated. I'd have taken the door off its hinges and waded into the fray without a second thought.

"Someone's in trouble," Lisa hissed in my ear. The expression in her eyes morphed from alarmed to calculating.

We both had a working arm, and really, what more did we need? Two on-the-run chicks to the rescue. I tried the doorknob, which turned in my hand. Unlocked.

Another pained wail raised the hairs on my forearms.

I glanced at Lisa and she nodded. I flung the door open and we barreled headlong into a short hall.

"Shoot me now!" the woman screeched. "Please. Ahh!"

We followed the screech into a living room in shambles. The couch and two side chairs were pushed up against the walls to accommodate a thigh-deep inflatable pool.

The screamer spluttered and thrashed, sloshing water over the edge.

Another woman, with dark, shoulder-length hair, dressed in black stood outside the pool, her hand on some part of the screamer's anatomy. It looked like she was pushing the woman under.

"Get her!" Lisa yelled, and we charged, taking the woman in black right off her feet. We sailed over the submerged chick. A piece of my brain registered the fact that our potential drowning victim was naked. Had we stumbled into some kind of weird sex act?

The thought flew out of my mind as I landed with a titanic splash beside the screamer. On top of me, I could feel Lisa and the would-be murderer struggling. The squirming bodies pinned me beneath the water. If someone didn't get off ASAP, I'd be a drowning victim myself.

I got a hand on the woman and shoved. She didn't budge. The urge to inhale became the only thing I could focus on. Then the weight on top of me was gone. The arm that was cuffed to Lisa was nearly yanked from its socket, springing me out of the water like a jack-in-the-box. I never truly knew until that moment how beautiful oxygen was.

Lisa had wrapped her free arm tight around the woman's neck, choking off her words. Spluttering, I scrambled to my feet and grabbed both of the attacker's wrists. Over my shoulder I yelled, "You're okay now. We got her."

Instead of a thank you, the would-be vic yelled, "What the hell are you doing? Let go of my—AHH!"

"What?" I twisted around, and my gaze locked on her bare belly. Her very large belly with a brown line running from just beneath her breasts, around her belly button, down to her pubic bone.

Suddenly everything became incredibly clear. "Holy shitcakes, Lisa! We tackled a midwife. Let her go!"

I whipped back around and looked down at the midwife, who was maybe five-two. Her black clothes were actually black scrubs covered with little pink ribbons. Dark, angry eyes met mine.

"I'm so, so sorry." I reached out and peeled a wet patch of dark hair from across the poor woman's mouth.

Lisa steadied her and stepped out of the pool. "We thought you—"

"The baby is coming!" the screamer bellowed. "The head! I can feel the head! Risa!"

Rivulets of water slid down the midwife's face as she quickly assessed the situation. She sloshed over to the woman and put her hand on her belly again. "Gretchen, okay. It's okay. You two," she barked, "help her out of the pool." Her eyes dropped to the handcuff binding us together. "Why—never mind. Just get her to the couch. Now."

We wrestled Gretchen out of the pool and held her up, puddles of water spreading over the shiny wood floor while the midwife spread a towel on the cushions.

"But I thought—OW!—I was going to give birth—AHH! At the hospital!"

Lisa and I looked at each other in terror and manhandled Gretchen to the couch. One of my greatest fears was that some pregnant woman would go into labor at the Rabbit Hole and wind up popping out the kid on the rug in front of the fireplace. For no rational reason, childbirth terrified me. Or maybe my fear was all too rational. That shit had to hurt like a son of a bitch. Which was why it was never going to happen to me.

Panic made my voice squeak. "Where's the phone? We'll call for an ambulance."

Risa scowled at us. "No, no, no. We can handle this just fine. This is a normal birth and we don't need an ambulance." The midwife turned her attention to her patient. She gently said, "Gretchen, honey, you've moved from active labor into the delivery phase sooner than expected. You're going to be fine." Then her voice turned cold. "Dumb and Dumber, my birthing bag is next to the TV. I need gloves, a bulb syringe and sealed scissors that are on the bottom right side. Then I need you to find me blankets, towels and a shoestring or piece of rope."

I made a beeline for the black bag. I'm not sure which way Lisa went, but it wasn't in my direction. With a yip, I nearly fell over backward. "Goddamn it, Lisa—"

"Sorry," she muttered and scuttled to my side. Together we crouched over the bag. I held it open while Lisa rummaged through various pouches of multiple sizes and shapes. Water dripped down my face, and I wiped my forehead on my soggy sleeve. This was definitely going to be recorded as one of the most non-live-downable moments in my life.

Lisa pulled out a baby boogie snot sucker sealed in a super sterile plastic bag and a packet of gloves and thrust them toward our attached hands. I grabbed the goods, and she fished around some more, coming up with a pair of silver scissors.

"Risa. Oh my God! Get this kid out of me! RISA!"

We handed off the items to Risa in a hurry.

"Gretchen," she said as she ripped open the packet and snapped on the gloves. "Breathe. You can do this."

The poor girl panted. Her face was tomato red and her eyes were wild.

"Dumb and Dumber! Towels, blankets and rope. Or twine. Or a shoelace if it comes to it. Now!"

Lisa and I exchanged another look. "Kitchen," she said. Discussing our movements beforehand was a good idea. In the kitchen, dirty dishes were piled in the sink. You can bet if I were the pregnant one, I'd be leaving all the grimy glassware and pasty plates for JT too. Not that I'd ever be caught dead pregnant. But JT as my spouse? That was an interesting and rather perplexing thought.

We snagged all the hand towels we could find and rummaged around for something resembling rope.

"D&D!" Risa hollered. "Where's the stuff?"

We hustled back into the living room and handed over the hand towels. Risa took one look at them and rolled her eyes.

"Blankets—" Gretchen stopped to breathe her way through a contraction then tried again. "Blankets," pant, "my bedroom," puff, "upstairs."

We found the stairway and left wet footprints all the way up to the first open door, which was the nursery. The master bedroom was behind door number two. A pile of neatly folded blankets sat on a chair in the corner, and I grabbed them all. "Now we need a rope," I said and looked frantically about as another scream issued from downstairs.

Lisa's face was as pale as Gretchen's. "Okay. Rope. If I were a rope where would I be?"

"Not in the damn bedroom."

"What about..." Lisa pointed at a charging cord wound around the base of a lamp on a nightstand.

"Grab it. Risa said a shoelace could work too." I propped a foot on the edge of the bed, sent a silent apology to Gretchen for dirtying the duvet. I gave Lisa some slack by holding my cuffed arm out and tackled my bootlace with the other without much success. Who knew a simple task could take on such difficulty with one appendage?

Lisa retrieved the cord and saw what I was trying to do. She closed the gap between us so I could use both hands. It only took three more howlings from Gretchen and I held the shoelace in hand.

We made a pit stop in the bathroom. I forced Lisa to turn her back on me and took the opportunity to finally go. The relief was deliriously delicious, but I didn't have time to enjoy it. Lisa ripped off a wad of TP and thrust it at me. I finished my business, washed my hands while Lisa grabbed an armful of towels. The plastic shower curtain caught my eye, and I ripped it down, sending broken plastic curtain rings flying.

Lisa ducked as one sailed past her head. "What are you doing?"

"Figured we could stick it under her. Might save that couch."

We thundered downstairs, my soggy sock slapping against the interior of my unlaced boot. I dumped the blankets behind the midwife and Lisa set the towels on top.

"Here." I held up the shower curtain. "I figured we could tuck it under." For the first time Risa's expression softened.

"Hey," Gretchen bellowed. "I'm right here, bitches. No need to—SHIT THAT HURTS!"

"Don't mind her," Risa said. "It's the pain talking. That's the first intelligent thing you two hooligans have come up with. Help me."

Between the three of us we smoothed the curtain beneath Gretchen and covered it with a clean towel. She leaned, hunched miserably over herself, against the armrest.

I grabbed the charging cord from Lisa and thrust it and my bootlace at Risa. "Will either of these work?"

"Yes. Thank you." She carefully set them on the couch within easy reach. "Gretchen, I know Brian is on his way from Red Wing, but I don't think the baby's going to wait for Daddy. These two girls are going to help you breathe, okay?"

"What—" Gretchen gasped, and I cringed with her as she panted through the pain. Then she managed "—ever. Just get this baby out. And if Brian—GODDAMN," she paused, fighting to take a breath, "tries to come near me ever again, I'll kill him!"

Risa's deep brown eyes locked on Lisa and then me. "Welcome to the world of breathing coaches. Go on and help her."

Lisa and I shifted the couch away from the wall to make room and awkwardly crowded around the end to kneel at either side of Gretchen's head. I had no idea what to do. I tried to think of shows where I'd watched someone giving birth and came up with zilch.

Gretchen inhaled, then bellowed, the sound nearly popping my eardrums. She pounded the cushion as she screamed.

"Breathe through it," Risa directed. "I'll tell you when to push."

Gretchen panted. I panted with her. Lisa did too.

"Okay," Risa said after a few rounds of non-pushing. "I feel the head. When the contraction comes, go for it."

I put my head by Gretchen's flushed cheek and whispered, "You can do this. I know you can."

Lisa grabbed Gretchen's palm and dragged our manacled hands to the arm of the couch so we could more easily brace ourselves.

Only a few seconds later the contraction hit. Gretchen first tried to breathe steadily, but the pain overtook her and she grunted her way through it. Then the grunts turned into a keening that abruptly ended, leaving us all rapidly sucking air.

"That's great, Gretchen." Risa's voice was even, her tone comforting. "You're doing great. A couple more pushes and you're going to meet your baby."

This time she went straight to a crystal-shattering howl that seemed to go on and on. I glanced at Lisa, whose face was contorted. It took a second for me to realize she wasn't grimacing in sympathy but was in real pain, and another moment to figure out the pain was caused by Gretchen crushing her fingers. I was glad I hadn't grabbed her other hand.

The contraction eased. "That's it, that's it. Good job." Risa placed a hand on Gretchen's stomach again.

We crashed through three more rounds of the same ear-splitting yowling before Risa said, "This is it! Push Gretchen! Hard!"

Gretchen listened well, starting with a low growl that blossomed into a long shriek. Her body shuddered, and then she collapsed.

"Here he is! Gretchen, here's your baby!" Risa laid the baby in all its wrinkled, blood-covered, white-gooey glory on Gretchen's stomach. "You have a little boy."

Mothers, daughters, sons and babies. My mom, Eddy and me. And Lisa, too, I guess. Welcoming a new being into this crazy world kind of felt like we'd come full circle.

Simultaneously laughing and choking on a sob, Gretchen gathered her son into her arms. Her sweat-soaked hair was plastered to her head and an expression of amazement was fixed on her face. I wondered if my mom had that same look of wonder when I was born. I'd never seen a more beautiful, bloody sight.

I gave Lisa a victorious grin. She returned a shaky smile and slithered limply to the hardwood.

CHAPTER FOURTEEN

After topping off the tank and picking up coffee, Mountain Dew and a big bag of Cheetos, JT and Coop hurtled south on I-35E. JT didn't activate the unmarked's emergency lights, but she hauled serious ass anyway. She'd made a couple of calls to cops she knew who worked the areas they'd be going through and told them she was on an emergency run. Luck held when neither asked what the run was for.

Before leaving the gas station, JT had checked in with Eddy. Without revealing the reason behind the need for almost five thousand dollars, Eddy had conned her friends into coughing it up.

Coop was off the hook.

JT explained what she and Coop were doing, and promised to be back well before the designated drop time.

As she drove, her mind churned through one scenario after another. But until they knew exactly where the drop was supposed to occur, the speculation was pointless.

They whipped through St. Paul without a problem and were now on a ridiculously slow 45-MPH stretch of the freeway. JT was doing an easy sixty, but then so were most of the cars. She shook first one hand and then another, trying to relax.

Coop broke the tense silence. "Can I ask you something?"

JT glanced at him then back at the road. "Sure. As long as it doesn't have anything to do with my sex life."

"Not directly." He grinned deviously. "When are you going to pop the question?"

JT's eyes widened. She cut him a sideways look to gauge whether he was dicking her around or not. His face reflected cautious earnestness.

It wasn't as if she hadn't thought about it. She was the one who'd invited Shay to live with her, after all. But marriage was a big deal. A really, really big deal. And it was so permanent. Well, mostly permanent if she didn't go all criminal and hack her spouse to death and then try to hide the body parts in various Dumpsters throughout Minneapolis. Jesus. She needed to get work off her mind.

"I—" She stopped and pressed her lips together. "Where did that question even come from, Coop? I love Shay. I do. With all my heart. But marriage? That's some serious shit right there."

"I know." He shrugged. "Rocky, Tulip, Eddy, Agnes, Lisa, Kate, Anna, Shay's dad, Jeremiah and I sort of have a bet riding on it."

"Are you freakin' kidding me?"

"Nope."

"I think I should be mad about that."

"But you're not?"

Was she? Her closest friends were placing bets on when she'd ask for Shay's hand in holy oh-my-God matrimony. But wait. What about Shay? Two people were in this relationship after all. "Who says I'm going to be the one doing the asking?"

"Shay's an underdog, odds on her are four to one. Personally, I'm sticking with the sure thing. Well," he cut her a calculating glance, "a pretty sure thing."

Holy fucking shit Batman and Robin. She found it next to impossible to think about marriage when her girlfriend was being held for a shitload of cash. The dread in JT's stomach doubled. With any luck, Shay would be okay at the end of this insane foray, and JT could actually contemplate proposing. Maybe. But for the moment, she had enough on her plate.

Maybe the bad guys would be there, wherever they were holding Lisa and Shay. They were deadly, geezerly ex-cons who didn't have a whole lot of intelligence independently. Or combined. That being said, they'd managed to kidnap two healthy, strong, capable women, so maybe she shouldn't write off their abilities so fast. That thought led her to wonder what they might be using for armament. What kind of weapons did they have? Knives? Guns? Something else?

One for sure, maybe both of them, had drug connections, and JT knew full well that they could be earlobe-deep in drug running, drug taking, drug selling by simply sitting in a jail cell. She held no illusions about the contacts they could have on the outside.

For the next eighty miles, Coop occupied himself by popping from one radio station to another while JT concentrated on conveying them to their destination in one piece while more useless scenarios ran through her head.

They opened the bag of Cheetos and demolished it. At least sucking the neon-orange off her fingers helped pass the time.

An hour and seventeen minutes after they began the run south, JT pulled into the Preston Motor Mart so Coop could relieve himself of the vast quantity of Mountain Dew he'd consumed.

JT topped the car off, paid for the gas at the pump with a credit card, and waited impatiently for Coop. In less than four minutes they were back on the road.

Coop now directed them with honest-to-God print maps since cell service had crapped out not far from town. Farms and open fields that would be green before too long dotted much of the land, and everywhere else thick forest crowded the road. Following Coop's directions, JT cut off on County Road 118, and then again onto a narrow two-lane road that twisted and turned through the forest and farmland.

"If I'm right," Coop said, "the driveway should be on the left right up ahead."

JT slowed, but didn't want to be too obvious in case the entrance was being watched. Shoulder-high brambles and spidery branches reached toward the car, and behind that barrier, trees towered in an imposing wall. From her vantage point the woodland looked damn near impenetrable.

"There!" Coop thrust his map at an indent in the bush. What had once been a dirt road was now a swath of tall brown grass swallowed by trees about twenty feet off the asphalt.

"You sure?"

"As sure as I can be considering this godforsaken place is out of range of any electronic device aside from a transistor radio. Google Earth made it look like the house was set back a ways, maybe a quarter mile in."

JT studied the sad excuse for a driveway. "It looks like someone's been through here recently. Look at how the grass is flattened." They rolled past the driveway and she sped up. The road meandered like a bendy stream. After a couple of minutes, Coop directed JT to pull off onto a gravel road leading to a primitive campground that, according to a sign tacked to a tree, was closed for the season.

"Leave the car here," Coop said, "it'll be out of sight. If we head in at an angle through the woods, we should be able to circle around the back."

"Guess I should have consulted you when I was trying to figure out our next move."

"Guess you should've, copper."

"Be nice. Sure you can keep us on track in the middle of the big bad forest?"

"I'm the best you got unless you want to tackle the trek yourself."

"Oh, no. I'm good in the concrete jungle, but out here? Are you kidding?"

"Let's do this then." Coop brushed a swath of pale hair out of his eyes. "Come on."

Ten minutes later, as far as JT was concerned, they were hopelessly lost. She had no idea how Coop reckoned their location when cell service was nonexistent and he'd left the hard-copy maps in the car. They'd probably freeze to death before they stumbled across their target.

They traipsed over fallen logs and forged through almost impassable undergrowth. She yanked an ankle through a patch of thorny bushes and wondered how the hell this land had been settled in the first place.

"Are we going in circles? I feel like I've seen that same thicket of pines before."

Coop peered around, then did a three-sixty and did it again. "I think we're okay. Come on."

Before long, they came across a car-sized path that wasn't more than two grooves running along either side of a raised hump. Here, too, the grass had recently been crushed by the passing of a vehicle.

"Driveway?" JT knelt next to one of the tracks and examined the broken end of one of the strands of grass.

"Could be."

She straightened. "Let's parallel this but stay out of sight. If we hear anyone—Coop, are you listening to me?"

"What?" He turned his attention to JT. "Sorry."

"Focus. If we hear anyone, drop like a stone, okay? And stay where you land."

"Drop. Check. Stay, check." Coop's brow furrowed. "What if I land on a nest of fire ants?"

"Fire ants?"

He shrugged. "Read about them in an ecology magazine."

"Aren't they hibernating right now?"

"No idea. The 'zine didn't get into that. Rocky'd probably know."

"Well, forget the ants and come on."

After that not much was said except, "Look out for that," or "Watch your step."

Why, JT mused as they hiked along, would anyone want to live out here in the middle of nofuckingwhere? The amount of time she'd been stuck in that tree house on the drug detail, and now this nature-filled expedition, solidified her appreciation for city life.

They reached a large clearing and hunkered down at the edge of the tree line. The path morphed into a dirt drive that ended at a clearing in front of a ramshackle barn. Not far from the barn sat a house. Years of bad weather had worn the paint away leaving grooved, dark gray plank siding. Part of the roof was collapsed, and most of the windows had been smashed. Both structures loomed lonely and forbidding. With luck, Shay and Lisa were somewhere on the forlorn property.

No vehicles were parked in front of the house but that didn't mean the men who'd taken Shay and Lisa hadn't pulled whatever vehicle they were driving into the barn or out of sight behind the buildings.

"Okay," JT said, her voice low, "you stay put while I take a look around." She unsnapped her holster and pulled her gun, then jabbed a finger at Coop. "Stay."

"Hey, I listen well when firearms are involved."

"Good. I'll wave you in when I know it's clear."

"Wait a sec." Coop snagged the back of JT's jacket, pulling her back down next to him. "Be careful. You can't exactly call for backup."

"I'm well aware. Just wait for me to give you a thumbs-up. If you don't see the signal in, say, fifteen minutes, haul your shit back to the car and get help." JT fished the keys from her pocket and handed them over.

"Got it." Coop gave her a solemn nod.

JT eased away and followed the edge of the clearing, taking care to stay within the trees. Soggy leaves muffled her footsteps, their smell lingering in the back of her nose. She'd much rather deal with the cloying scent than have to worry about every step crunching loudly.

The backyard was empty save for a few trees and an outhouse, its narrow door hanging crookedly within the frame. There weren't any visible electrical wires leading to the house or the barn. Maybe a line had been run underground. Or not. The land was rural enough that it was possible the power company never even made it this far out.

The door to the rear of the house was missing, giving JT a glimpse into the structure. The view was limited, but she could make out a couple of broken chairs, a lot of leaves and heaps of other unidentifiable debris. The place would make someone a good crack shack.

She made it all the way around the perimeter without seeing any signs of habitation. Another wild goose chase. Goddamn it. Time to clear the two buildings and get their asses back to the cities. She scanned the area one more time and then made for the barn.

The rolling door was partially open. She pulled a four-inch Stinger flashlight from her belt, holding it in one hand and her gun in the other. She peeked around the edge of the door. Daylight leaked through cracks in the roof, allowing enough visibility to see without additional light, so she tucked the flashlight away. Old, cobwebbed farming machinery was parked on one side of the barn. Horse stalls occupied the other. A hayloft overhead extended halfway from the back of the barn toward the front.

The air was dry and dusty. Once-golden straw was strewn across a hard-packed, earthen floor. She eased inside and cautiously checked each stall. The only thing left in them were feeders attached to the barn walls, their wooden fronts worn down by the chewing and scraping of countless bovine or equine teeth. Two rusting pitchforks, a shovel coated with something petrified, and a long-handled ax were propped next to a ladder of questionable integrity leading to the hayloft.

JT ascended as quietly as she could, hoping with each step up that the rickety thing would hold her weight. The loft was empty, save a lot of bird poop and a few bales of hay that had broken apart and settled in sheaves on the rough-hewn timber floor.

Back on ground level, JT holstered her gun and grabbed a pitchfork. She randomly jammed it into the soil in the very off chance a trap door was hidden under the mess. All she found were spiderwebs, a pile of ancient manure and three dead mice.

JT ditched the pitchfork and checked her watch. Six minutes to go before she needed to give Coop the all-clear.

She emerged from the barn and surveyed the yard. Everything remained unchanged, so she scuttled to three iffy steps leading to the front door. She had a foot on the bottom riser when Coop's muffled bellow stopped her dead. "JT! Hey, JT! Help!"

Heart hammering, she drew her gun and sprinted toward the sound of his panicked voice. "Coop!" she yelled as she skidded around the corner of the house. She heard him holler again, the sound muffled. "Coop, where are you?"

"Down here!"

"Where?"

"Down here, by the house."

Then she saw an exterior cellar that had been half covered up by the detached back door. She ran to it, flung the door out of the way and dropped to her knees. A cut branch maybe five feet long was threaded through one of the handles of two almost demolished swing-out doors. A set of stairs disappeared into hideous-smelling blackness. She put a hand over her nose and mouth. "Coop? Are you okay?"

"Yeah," he responded breathlessly, his tone less panicked. "Think so. I tripped over the door out there and pulled an Alice in Wonderland. Although this place sure isn't the Rabbit Hole."

"You fell down the steps?"

"Yeah."

"You hurt?"

"Twisted my knee, but otherwise I think I'm okay."

"I told you to stay put."

"I tried. Really I did. But I saw you go into the barn and figured I'd have your back and check the house. And then… never mind. What I really need is a flashlight."

With a curse, JT pulled the flashlight from her belt and reholstered her weapon. "I'm coming down." She pulled the branch free of the door handle and flung what was left of the doors open. The stairway shuddered beneath JT's feet as she descended into a rank, mold-infested cellar. The bright light from the Stinger bounced off damp cement and lit the area at the bottom of the steps, which, like the barn floor, was hard-packed earth. Coop lay sprawled against the wall.

JT held a hand out. Coop took it and bounded to his feet, only to smack his head on a cross brace. He yelped, ricocheted backward, bounced off the sidewall and landed in a heap. Right back where he'd started.

"Jesus, I'm sorry. Didn't realize the ceiling was that low." She knelt and pulled him into a sitting position. "Lemme see." She tried to pry his hands away from his forehead.

"Uhh."

"Come on, you baby." She grabbed a pinky and peeled a hand away as she shone the light on his hairline. A trickle of blood from a small gash made its way under his other hand and rolled down around his eye. Coop squinted at the bright light, pulled his hand off his head and looked at the palm.

"Yeah," JT said, "you're—"

Coop's eyes rolled back and he slipped to the ground like an overcooked noodle.

"What the hell? Are you kidding me?" JT muttered and sat back on her heels, still holding one of Coop's limp hands. "I thought you were getting better at this blood and guts stuff."

A couple of minutes later, Coop was back. One of his sleeves had parted ways with his sweatshirt and was now tied around his head like a bandanna. He very cautiously avoided the cross beams holding up the floor above and made his way to where JT stood in the middle of the ten-by-twelve foot cellar.

"How ya feeling, champ?"

"Don't ask."

"How much to keep quiet about your little fainting spell?"

"I prefer to call it passing out, and would fifty do it?"

"Maybe." JT flashed the light around. One end of a ten-foot pipe was ripped from the wall. Two stained zip ties lay on the floor. She nudged one of them with the toe of her boot, and then knelt for a closer look. "What's on them?"

Coop hunkered down beside her and picked one up. "It looks like—"

JT snatched the tie from him and slapped a hand over his eyes. "Breathe."

"What're—I'm okay." A bony hand grabbed her wrist and pulled it away. "Don't know what happened back there. I really have been better. I didn't keel when Shay's dad got shot." He squinted again at the tie. "Is that blood?"

"Could be. And see here," JT twisted the tie, "it's been cut. Doesn't mean Shay and Lisa were here, but it sure looks like someone was. Against their will."

They both stood. Coop cautiously avoided the brain-bashing beams.

"Let's get out of here." JT shone her light around the space one more time. "I'm at the end of my stench tolerance."

"Hey," Coop said, "what was that?"

"What's what?"

"Light up the space under the stairs again."

Something metallic reflected back at them. She edged closer. The blade of a knife was partially wedged beneath the floor and the bottom of the steps. She used the toe of her boot to scoot it out. As the knife rotated, light reflected off the handle, which was bright blue, with an intricately designed dragon. JT's pulse hit a thousand. She snatched up the object from the floor. A dark substance that JT was afraid was blood congealed in the grooves of the dragon. One side of the blade was engraved. "To Shay, may you always slay your dragons. All my love, JT."

She stood frozen, staring at the blood-specked knife.

"Be calm, JT, just like you told me." Coop put a hand on her shoulder.

She slowly closed the knife and pocketed it.

"Just because there's blood everywhere doesn't mean anything."

"I need air."

They fled the confines of the cellar. JT bent at the waist, hands on her knees, chest heaving as memories assaulted her. Shay, her light and love in a sometimes very grim world. Shay standing up for Rocky to a rude customer. Shay in bed, warm and wanting. Shay, filling her heart with the kind of unconditional love she'd never known before.

When she was sure she wasn't going to lose it, she stood and tilted her head to the now cloud-covered sky and considered what they'd found. "All right." Clear, midnight eyes focused on Coop. "Look at the evidence. Shay and Lisa were here. The sliced ties, the smashed cellar doors. They're probably on the run. And they're both resourceful."

"Which will take them a long way if Shay can put her homicidal feelings for Lisa aside. Who knows, maybe this will be a turning point for them."

"A constructive turning point forced by running for your life. Might work. Come on," she said. "They might be trying to call. We have to get back in cell range." She stalked toward the trees.

"Wait." In two steps Coop snared her arm and swung her in a one-eighty. "This way."

"Knew I kept you around for a reason."

CHAPTER FIFTEEN

"I don't get it. Still ringing through to voice mail." I gently hung up the handset attached to what seemed a three-thousand-foot cord, resisting the urge to slam it into the cradle like I used to do as a frustrated teen. The gargantuan curly-cord reminded me of the hours I'd spent wrapping a similar, although much shorter cord around my fingers while Coop and I bemoaned our adolescent years. Apparently the concept of cordless handsets hadn't made it into the boonies of southern Minnesota, which, according to Risa, was where we were.

This was the fourth time I'd tried to call JT between trips around the house trying to find the various items Risa needed. First she wanted a blanket for the kid from the nursery upstairs. Then she demanded we find Gretchen a nightgown and some slippers, so up we went again.

It was also the fourth time I'd eyed, through the kitchen window, an ax that was embedded in a tree stump in the backyard. A depleted cord of firewood was stacked nearby. A good whack of that ax would probably snap the chain between the handcuffs linking Lisa and me together and we'd at least be free of each other even if the silver bracelets remained.

Problem was, I'd tried to explain away our disheveled, handcuffed appearance by telling Risa and Gretchen we were participating in a tryout for the *Amazing Race*. I'm not sure they bought it, but they were too Minnesota Nice to question us. In my rapidly fabricated story, JT and Coop were heading up the tryouts, and in light of the situation, would come and retrieve us. In order to keep up appearances, we needed to leave the cuffs on.

Gretchen had recovered enough to slide into bossy mode herself and sent us to the second floor a third time to fetch Risa some dry clothes. Neither mentioned anything about Lisa's or my sodden attire, although I can't say I blamed them since we were responsible for looking like creatures from Swampville in the first place. For the most part the dripping was done, but clingy, wet garments weren't anything I ever wanted to spend much time in again. My underwear was riding up my ass and one sock had slipped down and was bunched under my foot, leaving my bare heel to chafe against the interior of my boot.

In the kitchen, Lisa hovered anxiously at my shoulder and I kind of wanted to elbow her in the solar plexus. "Call Eddy."

"It's not that I don't want to. I would love to warn her that Sheets the Shit and Bobby Knockers are off their rockers. I can't remember her flipping phone number or the number to the Hole. Stupid cell phones. Who remembers phone numbers any more? And who doesn't have home Internet?" No way could I live out here in desolation without Internet, cell service and no neighbors within miles. "If Coop or JT can come and get us, then we can warn Eddy. Preferably it'll be JT so she can get these shit-for-Sherlock cuffs off." I resolutely punched Coop's number into the phone again. That was one number I did remember.

"Girls!" Risa bellowed from the living room.

Lisa said, "Hang on, Shay's trying to call again."

"Keep it short. I have to suture mama up just the tiniest bit so I need some stuff out of my bag."

"Okay," Lisa said, watching my eyes.

Voice mail kicked in again. I'd already left numerous messages for both Coop and JT to call me back at this number so I hung up and we headed for Risa's bag of horrors.

Forty-five minutes and sixty-five or so errands later, the phone finally rang.

"Get it," Gretchen said absently, mesmerized by her new baby.

I made a dash for the phone, dragging Lisa in my wake.

"Hello?" I couldn't help the hopeful tone that leaked into my greeting.

"Who's this?" a man with a deep voice asked. For a moment I froze, mouth gaping, terrified the two leprechauns had tracked us down.

"Hello? Where's Gretchen?"

Oh, for the love of green beer. The likelihood of the Leprechaun Brothers knowing Gretchen had to be zero. I hoped. "Hang on," I said and we delivered the phone to Mom.

I tuned out the excited after-birth chatter and watched Risa do her thing with confident, efficient movements. She was cool under pressure, obviously loved what she did and cared deeply about her clients. If I ever got pregnant, which would happen when snowballs didn't melt in hell, I'd want Risa by my side. Just the thought of popping a kid out of my "down there" made me want to scream.

"Hey," Gretchen called out. "Someone beeped in. It's for you." She held the phone out to me.

About damn time. I grabbed the receiver. "Hello?"

"Shay?" The husky, heady sound of JT's voice washed over me like an illegal drug, leaving me simultaneously weak-kneed and suffused with warmth.

"JT. Holy cow, it's good to hear your voice."

"Are you okay? Is Lisa? Where are you?" The relief coloring her words told me just how wound up she was.

"We're a little banged up, but we'll live. You're not going to believe what happened. But before I get into it I need you to call Eddy and tell her to go to the Rabbit Hole and stay there no matter what. She needs to get out of her place and go somewhere there's people around."

"It's okay. She knows what's going on."

"What?"

"I'll bring you up to speed when we see you."

"Just promise me you'll call her as soon as you get off the phone with me."

"Fine. I promise. Where exactly are you?"

I gave her the address Gretchen had scribbled on my hand with a pen, and she relayed it to Coop.

In about three seconds I heard him say in the background, "We should be there in twenty, maybe less the way JT drives."

Now that rescue was imminent, both Lisa and I perked up. Gretchen conned us into holding the new baby, who she called Sneaky Pete since his name was Peter and he'd snuck out early. Hopefully he wouldn't take after my dad and sneak around drinking booze.

Not one to cross a mom who'd just delivered a nine-pound kid, I held him while Lisa cooed obnoxiously. No more than a quarter hour later, the doorbell rang. I returned the kid to Gretchen and opened the door to the glorious sight of my partner, her beautiful eyes wild and wide. Coop stood next to her, his mop of wheat-colored hair literally standing on end, as if he'd witnessed something truly hair-raising. Oh, man, they had no idea what was truly hair-raising. I launched myself at JT, forgetting, again, that I was bound to Lisa. Poor girl. JT peeled me off and released us from the cuffs. I rubbed my raw wrist, as thrilled to be disconnected from my sister as she was from me.

After a few minutes of leading explanations alternating between Lisa and me and confused glances from JT and Coop as we told our tall tale of being on *The Amazing Race* for the benefit of our hosts, we bailed. I was sure if Gretchen and Risa hadn't been so focused on Sneaky Pete they would have been on our lies like flies on yesterday's toast.

JT stuffed us in the backseat of her cruiser, mumbling something about soggy clothes and upholstery. Her squad wasn't set up for prisoner transport, so no Plexiglass or metal cage divided the front seat from the back. Unlike the front seats, which were cloth, the rear seats were covered with nasty Naugahyde so the detritus our filthy clothes left behind could be wiped up once we finally made it back to civilization.

I put a hand on JT's shoulder, on that spot close to her neck that I loved to nuzzle. After the trauma we'd been through, the need to touch her was almost overwhelming. She tilted her head and pressed her cheek against my hand.

By the time the tires hit solid pavement, which wasn't as far away as I'd expected, Lisa and I had brought Coop and JT up to speed on our so-called adventures, starting with the looney leprechauns, busting out of the cellar from hell, nearly getting caught by Bobby and Sheets and what little we'd learned from them, the ghost town, the murderer turned midwife and the harrowing birth of Sneaky Pete. As we talked, Lisa and I killed a container of wipes trying to scrub dirt and blood off various body parts.

JT said, "You're sure they mentioned someone named Scooter?"

I glanced at Lisa, who nodded and said, "Yeah. Sounded like a nickname for a chick, some big bad boss. Why?"

"I've just heard that name before. Now let me fill you in on what you've missed."

Between Zumbrota and Mendota Heights JT haltingly told a story possibly more bizarre than our own, involving a Brink's truck robbery and Eddy and an abusive, dishonest, thieving bastard named Leroy. When JT hit the part about Eddy blowing Leroy away, the Tenacious Protector inside me overcame my initial shock and raged. I trembled with fury.

Eddy, sweet, feisty Eddy, should never have had to go through that. She was more than salt of the earth. That woman was one of the most honest and real people I'd ever known. The tense silence that settled within the car practically crackled as I tried to process the implications.

Never in twenty-three million years would I think Eddy could have a secret so deep, so serious, so deadly. Holy crapping crackers. My Eddy had shot someone. She'd killed a son of a bitch who was beating the ever-loving tar out of her. And who'd beat Neil too. If that asshole Leroy hadn't beaten her to death that dreadful day, he probably would've at some point down the road. If I'd been in that living room with them, I'd have pulled that trigger myself.

JT caught my eyes in the rearview mirror. Hers reflected sorrow, love and something else I couldn't identify. Wariness? We lost the connection when she shifted her attention back to the road. "There's more," she said.

Trepidation burned its way through my veins, like how I imagined a hit of bad heroin might feel. I glanced at Lisa, then at Coop, who stared straight ahead out the windshield. He obviously wasn't about to turn around and face me. How bad could it be? My breath was hard to catch. "Did something happen to Eddy?"

JT barked a laugh. "No. She's fine." Her shoulders rose as she inhaled deeply. "It's about the accident you were in with your mom, Eddy and Neil."

JT was well acquainted with the reality of the single most harrowing day of my life. I still frequently woke her when I thrashed in the midst of a nightmare. The sounds were so vivid—squealing tires, rending metal, screaming. Oh, God, the screaming. I usually jerked myself awake during the screaming, feeling as if my abdomen had been sliced open only moments before, trying to swallow down the pain in my throat from hollering for my mother.

It probably wouldn't hurt to find another therapist one of these days, I told myself again. I'd been through a few over the years.

"Your mom," JT said, "was taking Eddy and Neil to the bus station...after what happened with Leroy. That was when your car was broadsided by the truck."

My mind raced, trying to suss out the meaning behind JT's words. My recollection of the events leading up to the accident was hazy. We'd been in a big hurry to get somewhere, that much I knew for sure. Then the next thing I was certain of was the moment I woke up in the hospital, sprouting tubes like antennae and feeling like someone had reached into my belly and ripped out every vital organ.

Vague impressions of the time between flashed through my mind, real or imagined, I wasn't sure. I was pretty confident I remembered sitting beside my mom as she drove, although I'd been told enough times that it was possible I'd morphed the recollection into a false memory. I remembered being so excited to ride in the front seat while another adult was in the car. Neil and I were usually relegated to the rear but this time Eddy insisted on sitting in back with Neil.

Now, after listening to JT recount what actually happened, I fully understood how desperately Eddy wanted to be close to Neil, how scared she must have been for them both and why I'd been in the front.

I fixed my eyes on the back of JT's head. I was in the here and now, not locked helplessly inside my own mind. At some point Lisa had put a hand on my forearm and now she gave it a squeeze. She didn't try to badger me with questions, but let me know she was there. I appreciated the gesture.

As my mind settled, I realized JT's unspoken implication. Eddy felt responsible for the deaths of my mother and her son. I repeated my thought aloud.

"Yes," JT said. "She does feel it's her fault."

Of course Eddy did. I would too, if I'd been in her shoes. But I could never blame her. "We were in the car because of Eddy, but it wasn't her fault some idiot blew a light and T-boned us. It was an accident." I felt physically sick at the thought of Eddy's pain, at the guilt she'd carried for so long. The urge to fix it, fix it *right now* nearly overwhelmed me.

"And then," JT said, and caught my eyes again in the rearview, sending silent strength to help me hold it together, "then we come to your leprechauns. Dwight Sheets and Bobby Temple. They were part of the armored car holdup Leroy masterminded."

Lisa asked, "Why did they snatch us?"

Coop threw an arm over the top of the seat, shifting so he could look back at Lisa and me without breaking his neck. "We now know what the 'it' is that they're after. Follow the armored car money."

"Sheets and Temple are pretty much your average, brainless, scheming felons," JT said. "They found Leroy dead in his living room and torched the place because they were afraid they'd be nailed for murder. Long story short, they were convicted— manslaughter and arson—and have been locked up for the last twenty-five years, give or take."

"Jesus." Lisa rubbed her forehead. "If I didn't already have a headache, this would do it. Coop says follow the money. What happened to it? Did it burn in the fire?"

When JT shot Coop a glance, that was enough awkward dancing around for me. "Okay, you two. Out with it."

"Eddy," Coop said, his voice deadly serious, "took the money. After she dispatched Leroy to the great beyond. The money is the 'it' they are demanding."

A moment of utter stillness filled the car, and then I burst out laughing. "Right. That's a good one. Eddy took the money. Sure."

"He's serious, Shay." There wasn't an ounce of humor in JT's tone.

"But—"

"She took it," JT said. "She paid your medical bills. Helped your dad when he needed funds. Used it to help buy her house. Helped you with your college expenses. Bankrolled the Rabbit Hole. The Leprechaun remodel sucked up the last of it."

I couldn't speak. Never would I have thought Eddy could kill someone. But she had. And it was completely out of context that Eddy would use dirty funds, someone else's money garnered from a robbery. But she apparently had. What would be next? At this rate it wouldn't surprise me if my homophobic father came out of the closet. The world's falling apart, I thought as I realized that every major monetary thing that touched my life in a substantial way before I was able to make my own dough came from heisted cash.

JT said, "According to Sheets and Temple, the money was gone when they found Leroy. They figured Eddy was the only one with access. She denied it, of course. But they don't believe her."

"They decided to use you two as bargaining chips," Coop said. "They're demanding ten grand by eleven tonight to keep you two alive, and the rest of it by tomorrow."

"We don't come cheap," Lisa said. "How much is the rest of it?"

"Actually," JT said, "you do come at a pretty good bargain. The rest of the haul was four hundred and ninety thousand bucks."

My eyebrows shot up so fast I could feel them nearly blasting off my face. Eddy spent half a million dollars on my father and me? "We should get into the heisting biz. Seriously, the point is moot now that we're free."

"Not exactly," JT said. "With or without you, they still think Eddy has the money."

"But she doesn't." I put my hands on my lover's shoulders and squeezed. Deep down I knew that little fact wasn't going to matter.

She leaned back at my touch. "They aren't going to believe it, and as long as they think Eddy has it, they're not going to let it go." JT tapped her thumbs on the steering wheel. "Therefore, we need to come up with a way to scare them off or set them on another track."

Lisa said, "Maybe we can convince them Eddy never had it."

"They kidnapped us. Wouldn't that send them back to prison?" I liked the idea of locking their leprechaun mask-wearing mugs back up. "But what kind of risk would that pose for Eddy? Could they rat her out? There's no statute of limitation on murder. I know that much."

JT said, "I don't know if they know who killed Leroy. I doubt anyone would believe two cons trying to finger a nice little old lady for a crime they were already convicted for."

The word "doubt" in JT's sentence worried me. I thought about Eddy and what she'd lived with for the last twenty-five years. If she hadn't needed to get to the bus station at that particular moment in time, it was very possible my mother would still be alive today. As would Neil. But, accidents happen, and maybe if it hadn't happened then it would have happened at another time. One thing I knew for certain: if I'd been in my mom's shoes, I would have done exactly the same thing to help a friend.

The fact that Eddy had spent so much money on my father and me was nothing short of stunning, and it helped make sense of some things. Like how my dad managed to pay bills on almost zero salary, how he'd made repairs to the Leprechaun when times were rough, how he'd been able to afford the basement repair and the upstairs redo. Pete O'Hanlon was a proud man. He'd never ask anyone for financial help. So that meant that Eddy had somehow conned him into accepting the money when things were at their most dire. At least he hadn't been stupid enough to turn his back on that.

The only interruption to the heavy silence weighing the car down was a phone call for JT. From what I could gather of the one-sided conversation, it was Tyrell, her work partner. Once she was off the phone she explained that whatever operation they were working was causing her supervisor to lose his mind and he was headed to wherever and whatever she'd been staking out this past week. She needed to get back before he showed up or the shit was going to fly. I knew JT wasn't happy to leave us to our own devices, but really, how much trouble could we get ourselves into?

Finally we were on Hennepin Avenue, and the familiarity of the shop-lined street helped settle me. JT pulled into the alley behind the Hole and parked in Eddy's minute driveway.

She pulled me in for a kiss before I crawled out of the car and whispered in my ear, "Wait for me to come back before you decide on any cockamamie schemes. I'll get out of this somehow as soon as I can." She cupped my cheeks and drilled me with her midnight gaze. "Please."

It was hard to say no to that. I wasn't so good at obeying direction, but what else could I do? "Okay." I planted a quickie on the tip of her nose and bailed. JT reversed into the alley and took off like a bolt of lightning.

I had a moment's hesitation, not knowing what to expect from this strange, new, slightly tarnished Eddy when she stepped out of the house. Her ebony skin looked pallid, but she held her head high. My concern melted away as soon as she pulled me into her arms and hugged the snot out of me. She must've been as afraid of my reaction to her as I was. So much for staying in the Rabbit Hole. Telling her what to do was about as effective as telling me what to do.

"Child," she whispered in my ear, "I'm sorry. I'm so sorry this has happened to you because of me."

I hugged her harder. "I know."

"We'll talk this through later, once things are squared away. I love you, and I always will." She rocked me back and forth like I was ten again, no matter that I towered over her by a good six inches now.

"I don't blame you for any of this, but I do have questions. So many."

"Oh, child. I know you do. And you will have your answers when we can sit down. And only when you're ready."

"I love you too, Eddy. You're everything to me, no matter what."

CHAPTER SIXTEEN

When trouble rose up and kicked us in the ass, it seemed like we always gathered around Eddy's kitchen table. The scent of cinnamon and vanilla that hung in the air centered me, and I sipped spiked hot chocolate from a chipped Rabbit Hole mug. Eddy called the concoction her sure-fire remedy for any problem. The "remedy" was a mixture of cocoa, one hundred proof Rumple Minze and a secret ingredient that I'd only recently learned was Jagermeister. Who'd have thought mixing hot chocolate and high voltage peppermint schnapps with booze that tasted like a cross between black licorice and Vicks Formula 44 would be palatable? No wonder everyone mellowed after they'd consumed a cup.

Eddy bustled around the kitchen in a lavender tracksuit and neon green high-tops, pulling together enough food to feed a troop of scouts. Between us, we polished off a loaf of bread, almost two pounds of summer sausage and a sizeable brick of cheddar cheese.

By the time I pushed my plate away and set aside my empty mug, relaxation was melting into mind-numbing exhaustion.

Thankfully, with the help of five ibuprofen, some of the aches and pains were diminishing. From the way Lisa drooped over her own mug, she was feeling the effects too.

Eddy surveyed us with an assessing eye. "Coop, Shay keeps a couple of changes of clothes in the Rabbit Hole kitchen, and I think there's some shoes and socks too. Can you please get them? I don't think this one," she poked my shoulder, "is getting up." Next, she appraised Lisa. "You'll fit into Shay's rags. Might be a little short, but that's okay. Kids these days. Why you hold on to pants with holes and sweatshirts with frayed cuffs is beyond me. I'll make these two honyockers presentable and then we'll talk strategy."

Honyockers? Where the hell did Eddy come up with some of the shit she said? No matter. Now that rapid-fire orders were flying out of her mouth, things felt a lot more normal. Or as normal as they were going to get considering the circumstances.

Coop fled for the change of clothes and Eddy sent Lisa off to shower in her bathroom upstairs. I took my turn, then we donned clean jeans, shirts that smelled like coffee and wonderfully warm socks and dry shoes. The only problem was lack of underwear. Usually underwear wasn't something that needed to be changed in case of a coffee shop mishap.

Eddy offered up her granny bloomers, but we politely declined, choosing instead to go commando. Wow. I didn't know how Lisa felt, but holy cowabunga, what an airy feeling down there.

Operation Cleanup accomplished, we regrouped in the kitchen. Chair legs scraped across the linoleum as we resettled around the table. Coop put both hands flat on the red and white plaid-covered surface. "Okay. What are we going to do about Sheets and Bobby?"

I'd opened my mouth to speak when Tulip and Rocky tromped into the kitchen. Tulip had a stormy look on her face. She crossed her arms and announced, "The two very naughty men should be strung up and tickle tortured to death."

Rocky's own expression was darker than I'd ever seen it. "Tickling will not cause death. They would die from starvation and dehydration instead, because I would not give them anything to drink or to eat after what they have done. While that might not be an economical use of our time, it would be worth it." He turned his attention to me. "Shay O'Hanlon, I am so very glad to see you." Then he launched himself at me, almost taking me right out of my chair. I grabbed him and Eddy steadied me before we all hit the deck. He righted himself, squeezed me again, and then targeted Lisa. Tulip remained in the doorway and watched Rocky's expression of exuberant affection with an indulgent smile.

"Pull up a chair, you two," Eddy said. "Might as well help us hammer out a plan."

Yeah, so much for my promise to JT. I'd make it up to her somehow.

I grabbed a glass bottle of Coke from the fridge and pried the cap off. It bounced off my knuckles and made a metallic ringing as it hit the counter, spinning like a top. That was how I felt. Like a top whirling out of control. "They know we're on the run but don't know we're safe and sound."

"How do they know that?" Eddy asked.

Lisa and I related the story of our nearly getting peed on.

Coop tossed down a toothpick he'd been chewing. "Bottom line—we have to somehow take Sheets and what's-his-name out of commission. Stop them from coming after Eddy again. How? Redirection? Is there a way we can make them think someone else swiped the money?"

"Hmph," Eddy said. "Those bozos don't know I snatched the dough. They might think I did, but they have no proof."

"Proof or not, Eddy," Lisa said, "they've fixated on you."

My bottle thumped on the tabletop as I set it down. "We can't go to the cops with this. It's too risky for Eddy."

"Coop," Lisa said, "do you have someone in your network who knows how to take care of things, if you know what I mean?"

"Like a mob hit man? I wish. Even if I knew someone, which I don't, stuff like that always comes back to chew you up. That's how you wind up a star in your very own episode of *Forensic Files*." Coop picked up his discarded toothpick and inspected the mushy end. "They're on probation, right? How do you go about getting it revoked?"

Rocky said, "Minnesota State Statute 609.14, Revocation of Stay." He leaned toward Tulip, cupped his mouth with a hand and whispered loudly in her ear, "It's about probation." He straightened. "It is not too difficult to revoke probation, my friend Coop. If the very bad men fail to submit to a drug test it can be revoked. If the very bad men move without letting their probation officer know it can be revoked. If the very bad men are charged with a new crime it can be revoked. If the very bad men have an appointment with their probation officer and do not present themselves it can be revoked. If the very bad men are supposed to appear before a judge or the court and fail to do so it can be revoked. There are other ways probation can be revoked too."

Lisa squinted at Rocky. "How does he do that?"

I shrugged. "Walking encyclopedia."

"No, Shay O'Hanlon. This time I am a walking website page called the Office of the Revisor of Statutes."

Eddy thumped the table with a fist, and I reflexively jumped, my heart pounding, stomach crawling with dread. Some PTSD counseling really and truly might be in my near future. On the heels of that thought came another. "I think I know what we can do."

"Oh, boy," Eddy muttered and rubbed her forehead the way she did when her head hurt.

I gave her a look. "Eddy, you and I meet with Sheets and Temple. Coop and Lisa stay out of sight, but close." I frowned at the wall, trying to follow the plan as it unfolded itself in my head. "This is going to completely depend on the meeting place they choose, I suppose."

"Hey," Lisa said, "if you guys can get them to confess to the armored car holdup, and to the murder of the guard, we've got them dead to rights. Right?"

"Yeah, absolutely. I think." Coop raised my hand for a high five. Lisa smacked it. I could almost feel the last of the animosity drain away that I'd stubbornly hung on to when it came to all things Lisa. We might be able to make a real go of this sibling thing.

"Coop," I said, "there's a voice memo thing on my phone, right?"

"Yeah. Sure is. But didn't Tweedledee and Tweedledum confiscate your phones?"

"Oh. Yeah. Forgot about that." I pursed my lips in thought. "You could be a nice pal and lend me yours. Then I could get the confession Eddy will squeeze out of them on tape. Well, not tape, but you know what I mean."

"Great idea," Eddy said.

Coop gave me a thumbs-up. "Anything for the cause."

"Okay. That'll work." I drained the rest of my pop. "Eddy, you'll have to lead them into confessing without implicating yourself."

"Bet your bottom buck I can do that. These two hooligans are going down." She banged a fist on the tabletop again. I jumped again.

Lisa put a steadying hand on my shoulder. "Once you get them to admit to killing the guard, try to keep them talking. Coop and I will move in and all of us will take them down. If they come armed, though, I'm not sure what to do. Play it by ear I guess."

"What about us?" Rocky asked, his heel banging steadily against the tile. "How can my lovely Tulip and I be of assistance?"

"Why, Rocky," Eddy said, "you and Tulip will have a very important role. You'll protect the car. We have to stash these two yo-yos somewhere once we got 'em under control."

Rocky gave her a salute.

Tulip said, "We are on the job for you, Ms. Eddy."

Eddy beamed. "That's my girl."

Coop said, "Speaking of stashing the yo-yos, maybe we should call JT as soon as we have them. If she can come with her squad, then we have a secure place to put them."

"Good idea, Coop. I'll lay out two options. Option A: leave town and don't come back, or I'll use the confession and JT can arrest them for murder. Eddy," I glanced at her, "how would you feel about giving them each a thousand dollar bank roll? I would think that would allow them to get the hell out of Dodge. And I'll pay you back."

"Sure, I can do that. A couple thousand bucks to get rid of those two dingdongs? Priceless. And you're not paying me back. What's their other option?"

"JT hauls them to jail, gives the confession to the US prosecutor and the case goes to the big boys. Minnesota might not have the death penalty but the Feds do. I heard JT and Tyrell talking about that a while back."

Coop grinned an evil grin. "Nice."

"The only problem," I said, "is that the jail option means the likelihood of Eddy's name being drawn into the mix is pretty high. That's why I think a little financial enticement for option A is the better choice."

The shrill ring of the phone made me jerk again. Jesus. Skip the therapy thing. I needed medication. Or more of Eddy's hot chocolate. That would probably take care of things.

Eddy grabbed the phone. "Okay," she said and jabbed her finger wildly at the receiver, mouthing, "It's them."

Beside me, Coop tensed. Everyone leaned toward Eddy as if she were a magnet and we were all made of metal.

"They what?" She listened some more. "I do not—" Eddy abruptly stopped again and listened for what felt like an hour. Then her brow furrowed and her eyes shifted from uneasy to sparking with fury. Uh-oh. From that expression I knew an explosion was brewing. I'd been on the receiving end of her displeasure enough times to know when she scowled like that, you may as well chew a hole through your lip rather than utter another word. Those two really had no idea who they were dealing with.

Eddy inhaled sharply, opened her mouth, then shut it so hard her teeth cracked together. Yup. Those dumbasses better duck because they were about to get it.

In a voice so quiet I could hardly hear it, she said, "Don't you dare come after a single one of them. You hurt any of my children, and you'll be one sorry mofo, Mister Temple. Good day." With that she slammed the receiver down hard enough it was a wonder she didn't rip the base right off the wall.

Yikes. When she used the mofo word, things tended to spiral out of control fast. Eddy stood facing the phone for a few seconds. Then she squared her shoulders and turned around. "They know the girls escaped, just like you said. They assume you're back home and if we don't hand over the entire five hundred thousand, they'll start picking off each and every one of you until I give it up."

"Picking off?" Lisa echoed.

I rolled my eyes. "Kill, Lisa." Maybe we did have some work to do with her yet.

"Oh." Lisa swallowed the rest of her hot chocolate in one gulp.

"And those dingdongs moved the timeline up. They want the drop at eight o'clock sharp under the bridge at Gasoline Alley. Said I should bring Shay and we have to park in the back of the lot and enter through a gap in the fence by the main building."

Coop glanced at his watch. "In forty-five minutes? At Gasoline Alley? That abandoned amusement complex in the 'burbs?"

"That's the one," Eddy said. "Haven't been there in years."

Lisa looked at Coop. "Where is it?"

"It's north on Central, might be Highway 65 that far up," he said. "Don't know exactly where, but it's on the left side."

"I remember that place," I said. "I thought the city demolished it a long time ago. It was near an old drive-in theater, wasn't it? Coop, Eddy brought us there to play mini golf and do the go-carts when we were kids. Remember? The building was white with stripes."

He shook his head. "I sort of remember, but not really."

Eddy said, "I did take you both there a few times. Then we went to that drive-in afterward. They had the best skin-on wieners in one of the most dilapidated concessions shacks I've ever seen."

Coop opened his mouth but Eddy added before he could speak, "No offense, Cooper, but men's memories hold about as much as a rusty shovel with a hole in it."

He shrugged good-naturedly.

"If we're all going to go," I said, "we should take my Escape. More seats."

Rocky said solemnly, "We will guard the car very well, Shay O'Hanlon."

"And," Tulip added, "if anyone tries to sneak up on us, we will sit on them until you return. And do not forget to bring the money, Ms. Eddy."

An idea I couldn't quite grasp kept niggling in the back of my mind. I closed my eyes, trying to capture the thought. What was I missing? Then it dawned on me we needed something to tie up Hocus and Pocus. "Excuse me," I said, and headed for the Rabbit Hole. It took a couple minutes of rummaging around but I found what I was hunting for and reentered Eddy's kitchen.

"Where did you go, child?" she asked as she rinsed the last of the mugs and set them upside down on the drying rack.

With a smug look I held up a handful of leftover zip ties from some long forgotten project and then doled out a few to each of us.

"Oh, yeah. Yes." From the tone of Lisa's voice she was on my page. "Couldn't be more perfect."

CHAPTER SEVENTEEN

The ride out of Minneapolis was a quiet one. City congestion gave way to swaths of suburban residential housing interspersed with strip malls where occupancy varied wildly. After a while, chain businesses replaced locally owned places: Chili's and McDonald's and Best Buy and Burger King and Home Depot. The trip felt a little like crossing into alien territory. Where were the mom and pop shops? The family-run cafés? The small bakeries serving long johns filled with creamy goodness?

Lisa drew me out of my sugar-inspired musings. "Shay and Coop, tell us what you can remember about Gasoline Alley."

My connection to the place was such a long time ago. "I recall a big round sign with a checkered flag. In the middle I think it said, 'Gasoline Alley Raceway.'"

"International," Coop said.

"International what?" Lisa asked.

"Gasoline Alley Raceway International. I remember that now. The phrasing was weird. Oh. The stripes Shay was talking about were red and orange and yellow. Painted on the building right below the logo."

I said, "Wasn't there an arcade in the concessions building too? Aside from the mini golf, racecars and bumper boats? Or was that Lilli Putt in Coon Rapids?" It felt like our visits out there happened in an entirely different lifetime.

"Hang on." Coop whipped out his phone. "Google Earth to the rescue." In about fifteen seconds he said, "Got it. Wow, I do kind of remember this. The parking lot is next to the mini golf, Shay. But man, is the place overgrown. Sad. I wonder how long it's been closed."

"The drop is under the bridge." I glanced at Coop then returned my gaze to the road. "Where's the bridge?"

Coop pinched and zoomed the graphics on his screen. "Yeah, that's right. I do remember now. Next to the mini golf area were the go-carts, or racecars as you referred to them, Shay. In one of the racetracks—holy crap."

"What?" Lisa asked.

"When Google passed over the property to take pictures they must have buzzed by in the spring or fall. So much green. Anyway, there's a bumper boat pool in one of the go-cart racetrack loops, and you can see the outline of three—no, four— bumper boats just below the surface of totally creepy, murky water. Disgusting. There could be a dead body under there."

"The bridge, Coop," I said dryly. "Where is it?"

"Oh, yeah. Okay. So you and Eddy need to follow the west wall of the concessions building. You'll be cutting through part of the mini golf area and you'll come out by the bridge. It looks like it goes up and over the portion of the track where they staged the riders at the beginning and end of a session. That's how people would get across the go-cart lanes to the bumper boats."

I glanced in the rearview mirror, but no one appeared to be tailing us. "Does it look like the bridge is made of something solid or is it metal grating? Can you see through it to the asphalt below?"

Coop turned the phone this way and that. "It looks like it's concrete. You certainly can't see through it."

"Good," I said. "Does it look like it's falling apart? Can you tell how high it is?"

"You ask a lot of questions."

I socked him on the thigh.

"Ow. Save your strength for the bad guys. Anyway, as far as I can tell it looks fine. Don't know how long ago these pictures were taken though. No idea how high it is. Do you remember?"

"Nope."

Eddy said, "Are you planning on leaping down on top of 'em like real superheroes?"

"Maybe," I said. "If Coop and Lisa can get up on top of the bridge it could work. They can drop down and squash Bobby and Sheets. If all goes well, though, we won't have to do that. I bet Eddy will be able to push their buttons enough to get them talking. Once we get the confession, Coop and Lisa can pop out and tell them they're surrounded. They don't know the two of them aren't cops. If Bobby and Sheets follow directions, we'll return the favor of zip-tying the lizardy leprechauns really, really tight. That shit hurts."

"I second that," Lisa said. "And if they don't listen, let's take 'em down."

I was totally down with taking them down. As painfully as possible.

The abandoned park came up on our left faster than I thought it would. We made a turn onto the residential road that bordered Gasoline Alley on the north end and continued down the street.

One side of the road was thickly wooded, and a mobile home park occupied the other side. A number of cars, probably belonging to the housing development, lined the wooded side of the road. I made a U-turn and slid into an open spot.

On his Google Earth app, Coop found a path he and Lisa could use to access the rear of the Gasoline Alley property. The plan was for me and Eddy to go to the meet-up spot under the bridge while our reinforcements snuck in the back.

The clock radio read 7:53. We'd made it with time to spare. It was in that moment that JT's words came back to haunt me. She'd said, "Wait for me to come back before you decide on any cockamamie schemes." Guilt bubbled in my guts, but I didn't feel like we had another option. I shoved the feeling down and killed the lights. "My one worry is that they're staking out the place and won't show if they see anyone but Eddy and me. We're going to wait a couple minutes after you guys leave to see if either of those two buttheads makes a move."

Tulip handed me something small and cylindrical that I realized was a flashlight.

"Thanks," I said. "This might come in handy."

"Don't use it unless you absolutely have to, Shay O'Hanlon," Rocky told me. "Stealth is our friend."

"Wait a sec." Coop handed me his phone. "Please bring it back in one piece."

"I'll do my best. At least if you need a replacement this time it isn't because it fell into the toilet."

Eddy groaned and Tulip giggled.

"I'm never going to live that down, am I?"

"Nope."

"Fine. Just wait. It'll happen to you too and man, you'll be sorry. So the voice memo's ready to go. Before you and Eddy go into the complex, all you have to do is hit the record button and keep the phone in your jacket. I turned off my security code, so you can just swipe it open."

"Okay." I pushed the phone into my pocket.

Coop and Lisa ghosted themselves away from the car and disappeared into the tree line. It was time, so I started the car.

Simply driving into an abandoned amusement park's parking lot spooked me, and we hadn't even set foot in the park itself. Streetlights were few and far between. When we'd passed the complex, I'd noticed there were no lights on the property either, which boded well for our improvised plan. I nervously patted the bulge in my pocket, reassuring myself that the flashlight Tulip had given me was still secure.

Random things I'd learned about Eddy in the last few hours tumbled through my mind as I followed the chain-link fence into the back of the parking lot. Some of Eddy's new reality was unbelievable, and yet some of it made perfect sense for the woman she'd become. I couldn't begin to imagine how she'd managed to deal with all she'd carried—by herself—for all these years. She was an incredibly strong woman.

Highway 65 bordered the east side of the compound, and even at eight at night a steady flow of vehicles rumbled past. The last thing we needed was to attract unwanted attention. If a curious passerby saw something and decided to swing in to investigate, it could be an epic disaster.

The parking lot was rectangular and narrow. Over the years, the untended asphalt had fractured into a spiderweb of weed-filled gashes, reminding me of the parched, cracked fields in Steinbeck's *The Grapes of Wrath*.

I backed into the corner of the lot beside a fence that bordered the mini golf section. Eddy and I exited the car and Rocky and Tulip moved up to the front. They were both dressed in black and wore yellow Minion ski masks pulled down over their faces. They'd make cute arrestees if they got caught.

Eddy stood outside the driver's door, talking to Rocky through the open window. She wore a black Windbreaker over the lavender track outfit. A fanny pack containing the bribery money was strapped to her waist, hidden by the nylon Windbreaker. Eddy's legs looked like vivid purple pencils, and her feet were encased in those damn neon green high-tops. Clutched tight in her hand was a mini Minnesota Twins baseball bat she called her Whacker.

I leaned into the window and whispered, "You two look like a couple of ninjas."

"We are not ninjas, Shay O'Hanlon," Rocky said and rolled his eyes at me.

"No, we really are not," echoed Tulip. "I am Minion Tulip and he," she jerked her thumb at Rocky, "is Minion Rocky."

"Okay then, Minions." I gave the windowframe a tap. "Guard the jalopy."

"We will be sure to take care of your jalopy, Shay O'Hanlon," Minion Rocky said, his hands at the ten and two position on the steering wheel. He wiggled it excitedly back and forth. I didn't think he knew how to drive, and I felt my pocket to make sure my keys were safely tucked away.

"Can you two breathe through those masks?" I asked, vicariously feeling my face itch. I hated the feeling of damp wool against my lips. It was probably caused by too many scarves wound around my head in the winter. I'd often looked like Ralphie's poor kid brother in *A Christmas Story*.

"Yes, Shay," Minion Tulip said. "A little bit of cloth will not impede our ability to breathe. We are on the job."

After Eddy gave the two some final instructions, we struck out for the abandoned concessions building.

I pulled out the flashlight and the phone and realized I hadn't started the recording. "Shit," I muttered and tapped the red dot to get it going. Then I stuck it in the pocket of my hoodie. I whispered, "We just need to get a confession."

"I know the plan. I was there, silly girl." Eddy gave me a poke with her bony elbow. "How are we supposed to know when everyone's where they're supposed to be?"

"I have no idea."

She harrumphed. "That's about how these things go."

The wire mesh fence next to the building had been snipped, allowing a person to pass. Eddy and I slipped through the gap into a bramble patch that was once a mini golf hole with a windmill feature. The poor windmill wasn't much more than a skeleton. One of its four slatted blades was missing, probably broken off by vandals and reclaimed by the encroaching land.

We followed a narrow trail of uneven concrete between the building and the out-of-control undergrowth. Just as Coop said, the path opened to the pit area where go-cart drivers had once lined up before and then again after their allotted laps.

To our immediate right, a set of steps led to a footbridge spanning the stop-and-go pit on one side and a go-through lane on the other, which, if memory served, racers employed to bypass the pit until they were flagged in when their time was up.

The first third of the stairway was choked with a creeping, vine-like growth. If the opposite side had the same problem, Coop and Lisa would have a real challenge accessing the deck. So much for Superman making an appearance. The good news was that to my untrained eye, the infrastructure looked solid, but then again so had the I-35W bridge right before it collapsed into the Mississippi in 2007.

To my left, maybe twenty-five feet into the pit area, a wheel-less go-cart rested on its side on the track. It looked like it'd been torched. Not far from the wreckage was a white, dome-shaped object that would probably fit into the circle of my arms. Behind the go-cart was another cylindrical object made of mesh.

The space below the bridge was devoid of the two loathsome leprechauns.

Eddy said, "You should take that lid and put it on the garbage can over there. Neaten up the place a titch."

Jesus. A simple garbage can and lid took on a whole different dimension in this creepy place.

"Hey there, sweetheart," a voice called. "You made it."

I nearly gave myself whiplash. Sheets and Bobby stood on the tarmac in the shadow of the bridge. Blood rushed to my head. It was really hard not to go after them then and there. Damn impulsivity.

Sheets, the short one, said, "Look who's here. Found your way out of the woods, huh? So, Eddy, that girl of yours there, she Leroy's love child?"

I clenched my fists in fury.

"What?" Eddy said with a frown. "Leroy's love child? Do you need a pair of glasses?"

Bobby smacked Sheets with the back of his hand. "Shut up. Come on over here, ladies. Wouldn't want to draw any attention to our little transaction, would we?"

Chanting the word "control" to myself, I reluctantly trailed Eddy as she marched toward the two men. Other than the sound of passing vehicles in the distance, all was quiet. Hopefully our backup was at hand, because I had the feeling the shit was about to hit the broken windmill.

"Bobby," Eddy said, "you really need to do what you did?"

"What's that, sweetheart?"

"Was it necessary for you two dumb-dumbs to kidnap Shay and Lisa?"

"Hey." Bobby threw his hands in the air. "Dumb-dumbs. That's funny. No hard feelings, right? We needed to get your attention." He jabbed a thick finger at me. "And you. You and that hellion escaped before we could have fun anyway."

I may have growled. I vacillated between biting my tongue and letting him have it.

"You listen, Bobby." Eddy stepped forward and wagged the Whacker in his face. "You keep my girls out of this business. This here mess is between you and me."

"And me too."

Eddy huffed. "Yes, and you too, Sheets."

"Now, sweetheart—"

"I told you to stop calling me that, Bobby. I'm not your sweetheart."

Sheets elbowed Bobby. "You always wished she was your sweetheart."

"Shut up, Sheets."

"You did."

"Shut. Up."

Seriously? At this late date, there was some sort of unrequited love triangle from the past coming back to haunt Eddy?

"Well, you did," Sheets said. "You told Leroy he didn't deserve her."

"He didn't—Jesus, Sheets. Shut the fuck up."

I rolled up my invisible sleeves. Time to give the cauldron a stir. "Did you have a crush, Bobby?" I asked.

"Never you mind. Now, Edwina, where is the money?"

"I told you. Don't have it. Never did." Eddy jammed her fists on her hips.

Sheets said, "You were the last one to see Leroy. He had the cash from the armored car. He told us to give him a couple hours so he could talk to you, and then we'd divvy up the dough. You offed him and ran with it."

"How do you know I saw him at all, you old gas bag?" Eddy's ornery meter was cranking up.

"Leroy was all hot to tell you what went down," Bobby said. "He didn't exactly have any other girlfriends to share the news with."

"How exactly, Bobby, did it all go down?"

Go, Eddy.

"Oh, come on, sweetheart," he said. "You went over to his place. He told you how we knocked over the truck. Showed you our haul. Then, although I have no idea why, you killed him and ran off with our hard-earned loot."

"How many times I gotta tell you? I did not see him that day." Eddy shivered and hugged herself. "But I've always wondered if he was the one who did that guard. Was always proud thinking my man took care of business."

Nice bait.

Sheets laughed. He said, "Leroy was good at beating on women, not so good at taking care of biz. That's what Bobby does. He always takes care of biz."

"Yeah, Eddy." Bobby's tone shifted from brusque to something softer. "I'm the one who takes care of business. All kinds of business."

I thought I heard something clang nearby. I tensed, but no one reacted. The urge to look around was almost irresistible.

"Right, Bobby." Eddy's tone was sarcastic. "It was Leroy all along, wasn't it? He planned the heist, pulled you two in, and dealt with whoever got in his way. He was a real man."

"No!" Bobby bellowed, rising to the balls of his feet. "Listen to me. Leroy might've bragged to you that he planned the hit on the armored car, but it was me. All me and nobody else. I was the one who told him to get to know you better. I was the one to tell him what to look for when he conned you into taking him into your bank. I drove the car, I shot the guard. I did it. Me. Not Leroy. He was nothing but big and dumb. An animal. Ask Sheets. He was there. I was the mastermind. Down to the last—"

Whatever words were about to come out of Bobby's mouth were ripped away as Lisa and Coop charged out of the darkness, screeching like escapees from an insane asylum.

Eddy yelped, leaped backward like a startled gazelle.

Lisa body-checked Sheets and jumped on him. He stumbled to his knees and bounced up as if he'd gone down on a trampoline. She hung off his thick neck, trying to knock him off-balance.

Eddy recovered and bolted for Sheets and Lisa, Whacker raised. I shot toward Coop and Bobby.

When Coop hit him, Bobby wobbled and almost kept his footing but Coop's momentum was too much. He crashed forward onto the track.

Bobby bellowed like a bull with his balls in a vice, and shook Coop off. Pushed himself to his knees.

I took a running leap, landed on his back. Hooked an arm around his throat like Lisa had done with Sheets. He staggered to his feet as if I weighed nothing, desperately trying to pry my arm away. I squeezed harder. How long did it take to make the sleeper hold work anyway? Too bad I hadn't Googled that in advance.

Coop stormed back into the melee.

The sound of a sharp crack echoed against the chipped concrete surroundings.

Sheets squealed, then hollered, "Eddy, ow! My shin!" I glanced over my shoulder to see him hopping around on one leg as he tried to simultaneously grab his right shin and dislodge Lisa.

Balancing on one leg is hard enough, but impossible with an extra hundred and fifty pounds of squirming Lisa attached. He slowly crashed over like a falling redwood tree.

My attention was brought back to Bobby as he tripped over the top of the garbage can Eddy'd pointed out earlier. Down we went.

Coop grabbed one of Bobby's wrists and dragged it behind his back.

I grabbed the thumb of his other hand used it like a joystick to guide it toward the hand Coop held and we zip tied him. I cranked that sucker tight.

"Hey," Bobby hollered. "That hurts!"

Eddy loomed over Bobby's head. "Help Lisa. I'll take care of this one." She tapped Bobby on the back of the head. "He moves and I'll really pop him."

Coop and I scrambled off Bobby and bolted toward Sheets. Somehow he was back on his feet, staggering in drunken circles. He made weird mooing sounds as he tried to divest himself of Lisa, who now hung onto one of his arms for dear life. Coop glommed onto his back like an obscenely huge wood tick, arms around his head and ankles locked around his broad middle.

I dashed into the scrum, grabbing Sheets's upper arm.

He roared, we all spun faster.

The momentum of this impromptu game of crack the whip lifted Lisa into the air like a rag doll.

Sheets gyrated toward a bridge pillar, slammed Lisa's legs violently into the concrete. The force of the collision broke her hold. She landed hard.

I ducked a meaty fist he jabbed at my face. It grazed off my shoulder and threw him off-balance. I let go of his arm and shoved him in the chest hard as I could. He tottered, then fell onto his back on top of Coop. Together they looked like an upside down Ninja Turtle.

With a growl, I tried to wrestle him off Coop. The guy might be compact but he was built like a brick shithouse.

"Help!" Coop's voice was high-pitched. His arms were still locked around Sheets's throat. Even flattened like a flapjack, he had game.

Sheets bucked like an enraged bull, sending me sprawling. The only thing keeping Sheets down was Coop clinging to him. I scrambled back into the fray, tried again to shove him off Coop.

Then I heard the crack of Eddy's Whacker. Sheets stopped fighting and yowled, "My head! She broke my head!"

White static fizzed in my brain, buzzing so loud I couldn't hear anything anymore. All I could focus on was removing him from my best friend.

Together Eddy and I rolled Sheets off Coop, who peeled himself from the concrete and helped us shove the squalling man the rest of the way onto his belly. I grabbed one of his wrists, using my body weight to keep him from jerking it out of my grasp. Coop got hold of the other mitt and between the two of us we wrestled his arms behind his back.

Eddy moved in with three ties—one for each wrist and one to connect the two since no way were his hands going to meet—and made short work of zipping up Biggie Boy.

Eddy lurched to her feet, panting. "Good thing...I had lots...of those plastic...thingamajigs." She pointed the Whacker at Bobby. He was still on his belly, arms secured behind his back. One leg was bent at the knee and his ankle was connected to his wrists by a succession of three looped-together zip ties. "Holy patootie."

Coop said, "We got a confession and we got the bad guys. The ghosts of Gasoline Alley are waving the checkered flag."

CHAPTER EIGHTEEN

I called JT, and she was already headed back to Eddy's, about five miles from our location. I diverted her to Gasoline Alley, but didn't explain why. I told her to go past the abandoned park and to where I'd let out Coop and Lisa, across from the mobile home court and text me when she arrived. She agreed, but there was a definite note of suspicion in her voice. Boy, was I going to be in trouble.

Bobby and Sheets were now zip tied to one another by one wrist and one leg. Each of their other wrists were zipped to the chain-link fence in the farthest corner of the lot where vegetation sprang through the wire mesh, providing us a little bit of cover from the busy highway. It was as secluded a spot as I could find nearby, and hey, paybacks were a bitch anyway. As an added precaution, I'd attached the garbage can lid to Bobby's other ankle like an impromptu ball-and-chain. They weren't going anywhere.

Eddy loaded Coop and Lisa, along with Minion Tulip and Minion Rocky, into the Escape. Both the Gasoline Alley

Avengers were pretty banged up, and Doctor Eddy proclaimed it time for a trip to the ER.

I was worried about Lisa. When she'd collided with the pillar, something popped in one of her knees and it wouldn't support any weight. After all we'd been through together, I knew her pain tolerance was pretty high. From the grimace on her face, I knew she was hurting pretty damn bad.

Coop's arms and a cheekbone had bruises emerging. He complained that his right side hurt like hell. I wondered if maybe Sheets had broken a rib when he landed on top of him, and that could lead to a whole mess of trouble. I was glad when Eddy revved up the engine and hightailed it toward the emergency room. Before she left, she handed over her cash-filled fanny pack to me.

As Eddy's taillights faded from view, JT came charging around the far corner of the lot, zigzagging her way across the crumbling parking lot toward us. I hadn't even noticed her drive by.

She skidded to a stop and looked from me to our trussed turkeys. When she looked at me again her eyes were slits. Through clenched teeth, she ordered, "Over here," grabbed my arm, and dragged me a few feet away. "Holy shit, Shay. What the fuck is going on?"

I swallowed hard. She really wasn't happy. I rapidly filled her in on the phone call from Bobby and our scheme to capture the confession. Thank God the phone hadn't been damaged in the brawl. We'd checked it before my partners in crime left, and, while it was somewhat muffled, every word had been recorded. That was the ammunition I'd used to keep Bobby and Sheets from screaming for help like a couple of babies.

JT did a few deep breaths and pulled herself back together.

Once she cut the sullen twosome loose, we marched them down the dark street toward the squad, away from the Last Stand at Gasoline Alley. I figured our showdown was the final gasp of excitement the long-forgotten venue would see until the bulldozers showed up.

"Okay, guys," JT said when we reached the car, "in you go." With a little prodding they complied and she slammed the door behind them. Then she roughly pulled me against her. Here it came. "That was an idiot move. You could have gotten yourselves killed. What were you thinking? Jesus freaking Christ." She closed her eyes, leaned her forehead against mine. Then, "You okay? Did they hurt you?"

I still trembled from adrenaline overflow and my head ached, but that was small beans compared to Lisa's and Coop's troubles. "I'm fine." I hurriedly explained what we needed to do next to move this scheme along, then slid my hands inside JT's jacket, my palms on her warm sides, hoping that would help keep her calm.

"I'm impressed with your deviousness. Good job."

"Thanks. It was a group effort," I whispered, relieved she was going to go along with the plan. "I know what a risk you're taking."

"Shh." She stopped me with a finger to my lips. "Later. Let's walk these jokers through their fantastic offer and make tracks for the bus station."

JT and I settled in the front seat. She started the car and fired up the heater. Then we turned around to face the morons in the back.

"Listen up, you two," JT said. "Here's the deal. I'm only going to propose this once."

Both men stared straight ahead.

"You've got two choices," JT said. "You know Shay recorded everything you said back there."

I couldn't quite make out Sheets's muttered oath.

"I can haul you down to the station, make a call, and turn you over to the Feds right now. Thanks to your confession, they'll charge you with murder. Minnesota doesn't have the death penalty, but the Federal Government does." She paused to let that soak in. "Or, I can give you a thousand bucks each and buy you a bus ticket anywhere outside Minnesota you'd like to go."

"What's the catch?" Bobby asked, his gruff voice flat.

"The catch is that you never cross the border back into this state, and never try to contact any of us, especially Eddy Quartermaine, again."

Sheets snorked up a giant loogy and swallowed noisily. He asked, "Why are you offering us this?"

"Sometimes," JT said, "it's better to skip the questions and accept what's being handed to you for the gift it is."

Bobby asked, "What about our probation situation?"

"Not my problem," JT said. "Stay out of trouble and you won't have an issue."

A loud knock on the driver's window made me hit the roof. Well, maybe not literally, but almost literally. I might've squealed and I dropped the fanny pack on the floor. Someone shone a light through the glass. I squinted and put up a hand to block the glare.

JT muttered, "Shit," and rolled down the window.

"What's going on here," a female officer asked.

My heart bypassed my throat. I had instantaneous visions of all of us in orange jumpsuits being led away in handcuffs. I knew this evening's events had been working out way too easily.

"I'm with Minneapolis. Homicide." JT handed over her identification, which she'd already pulled from a pocket. The cop flipped the case open and studied the badge and credentials for what felt like twenty-six and a half minutes.

I glanced back at our prisoners and waggled my phone at them. Sheets ignored it, but Bobby narrowed his eyes and his face twisted, though he kept quiet.

She finally handed JT's badge back. "Bordeaux, I've heard of you. What's going on this far out of the big city?"

"These two are staying over in the mobile home park and claim to have some information we need for a case we're working. Just going to run them downtown for a chat."

The officer grinned. "Don't be afraid to give us a shout. We're happy to help anytime."

"Thanks. If it were any more serious, I'd have given your dispatch a heads-up."

"Okay. I'm out here till twenty-three hundred." She pulled a card from her breast pocket and handed it over. "Give a call if you need anything."

JT saluted her with the card. "Will do."

The cop tapped the roof twice and walked away.

My heart started beating again when JT rolled the window up. "Jesus Christ," I said, "let's get the hell out of here."

She shifted into drive and pulled out. "The fun never ends."

We'd only made it to the end of the road and turned onto 65 when JT's phone rang. She answered, "Bordeaux," swapped the phone to her other hand, and listened for a moment. "But—yes, sir." Then she listened some more.

The car slowed, and JT squinted out the window, looking for something. "Okay. I'm on the way." Her tone was resigned. There were a few more "uh-huhs" and "yeahs" and "yes, sirs" before JT disconnected and muttered, "Fucking Malachuk." We slowed more, and suddenly we were whipping a shitty across the median. The engine roared as JT floored it.

Sheets shrieked. "You trying to kill us back here? How come we ain't got no seat belts? Shit, these fucking zip ties hurt!"

The rear end fishtailed as rubber fought for traction. I thrust my arm up so our backseat passengers could see the abrasions they'd caused on my wrist. "Suck it up." I wanted to add, "dickhead," but refrained. To JT, I said, "What's going on?"

"The team is moving on the target now. The man in charge figured out pretty quick I'm not there. Told me to stop shitting and double-time it back so I can help with the house-clearing, drug-hunting after-party."

"Stop shitting?"

"Don't ask."

"They want you right now?"

She toggled a couple of switches. The sudden blast of the siren above my head startled me. Metal road signs reflected the red and blue and white of the emergency lights she'd activated. "Yeah, right now."

* * *

Fifteen minutes later, we bumped down a tree-lined, rut-filled drive that opened onto a huge yard filled with so many emergency vehicles and flashing red and blue lights it made me dizzy. JT pulled off the drive and angled alongside a black SUV.

"Stay here," JT ordered. "I'll be back as soon as I can." She squeezed my hand and exited the car. A second later the trunk popped and then the car bounced when the lid was slammed shut. JT hurried past, pulling on a Kevlar vest. She stopped someone and they exchanged a few words. Then she angled toward the front door of the house and disappeared inside.

Man. The timing on this sucked pickled eggs. We were so freaking close to disposing of the two rat-shits in the back, and now who knew how long before JT and I could get rid of them.

Law enforcement types swarmed like ants in every direction, some leading handcuffed suspects to waiting squads. Various Windbreakers and body armor designated FBI, DEA, SHERIFF, SWAT, POLICE and probably other agencies I hadn't seen yet.

My shoulders were tense, making my headache worse. I wondered if some fresh air might help. "You two stay put," I said with a rancorous laugh and climbed out, not too worried because JT's back doors didn't open from the inside. My insides felt like they were screaming. I just wanted this whole goddamn thing over with.

The air was cold and I pulled a deep, cleansing breath. My body felt like it was crying I was so tired. But we were on the home stretch, and I just needed to dig deeper to find a little extra energy and patience. Might as well take in the spectacle of the bust. And what a spectacle it was. I'd likely never have another chance to witness a drug operation or whatever this was being taken down.

Pandemonium reigned. Radios squawked, people shouted, and everyone was on the move.

I wandered to the front of the car, leaned against the hood, and crossed my arms. Holy crap on a ginormous cracker, a lot had happened in the last twenty-four hours, give or take a few. In one fell swoop, many of the beliefs I'd held close to my heart about my family had been stripped away, leaving a strangely hollow space in my gut.

Certainly I didn't blame Eddy for my mother's death, but I knew she blamed herself. The one-two punch of losing a best friend and a son would have been the death knell for someone less resilient.

And then there was Neil. Between losing my mom and my own surgeries, subsequent recovery and the changes in my life after that, it occurred to me in that very moment, amidst the chaos and flashing lights, I, too, had lost a good friend. I'd mourned Neil after he died, but until that moment, never realized how much he'd really meant to me.

Eddy had always been my straight shooter, pulling no punches and telling things like they were. She'd been that way with both Neil and me. After the accident, she'd taken over watering the ethical seeds my mother had planted, nurtured my ideals of right and wrong, of helping others, of what loyalty and love meant.

Now that Eddy's truth was exposed, did that change anything? Did the fact that illegally gained money had touched almost every facet of my life matter? I could rail and scream and spew all sorts of righteous anger, but in the end, what difference would it make? It wouldn't bring my mom back, wouldn't bring Neil back. It wouldn't change the fact that Eddy had done what she had.

The feel of ice-cold metal seeping through the fabric of my jeans stirred me from my inner musings. So much adrenaline was pumping through me that I hadn't felt the chill in the air until now. A shiver snaked from the back of my neck down my spine.

The car bounced against my butt, and for just a second I was awed that I shivered hard enough to shake the heavy vehicle. The car rocked again, and in that moment I realized no shiver would have caused that kind of movement.

I whipped around. The driver's door was open. Bobby was struggling to his knees in the dead grass a few feet away. Sheets tumbled out of the car, then tried to heave himself upright. Not easy to do when you're short and round and your hands are tied behind your back.

For a fraction of second I was too stunned to move. "Hey," I shouted, then rocketed around the front of the car. Bobby staggered backward out of reach so I made a dive for Sheets. I hit the ground with a thud and I snagged his pant leg.

He kicked at me and yanked his leg forward, ripping himself out of my grasp. He popped up like Jack leaping out of the box and ran awkwardly after Bobby.

"Oh, come on!" I yelled and clambered to my feet. Bobby had maybe a hundred foot lead, and Sheets fifty. My advantage was the use of my arms, and I pumped them hard, flying around three squads and an ambulance.

I thought one of the many cops swarming the place would join in the chase until Bobby veered to the outside perimeter of the farm, avoiding the majority of police activity. He circled around the side of the house and headed toward the back, where he disappeared.

I was closing in on Sheets, who took a more direct line toward the back of the two-story house than Bobby did. He cut the corner too close and caught the edge of the structure with his shoulder. The force of the impact spun him in a circle and then he was moving again. I gained a couple strides and screeched around the corner on his heels.

Sheets was only a few feet ahead of me. Bobby was across the yard, paralleling the corn, run-waddling as fast as he could. Light blazed through windows at the rear of the house, brightening the narrow backyard. A massive field of uncut corn pressed in close, its crunchy-brown six-foot stalks rustling loudly in the breeze.

A fleeting thought that Lisa would be happy she wasn't here dealing with another cornfield popped into my head as I gained another foot.

With a roar, I launched myself at Sheets, catching him around the waist. My momentum spun him sideways, and then the world blew up.

CHAPTER NINETEEN

JT dove into the inevitable semiorganized chaos that came on the heels of a raid, velcroing herself into her vest as she scanned the yard for familiar faces. If she could find Tyrell, she knew he'd do what he could to redirect Malachuk's attention from her long enough that she could deal with Sheets and Bobby and get her butt back to the bust. After this, she owed her partner seriously freaking big-time.

She recognized a cop hustling past and caught his arm. "Hey, Salvo, you seen Tyrell Johnson?"

"Bordeaux, where you been? You missed all the fun."

If only he knew how much fun she was trying to juggle at this very moment. She bounced on her toes, hopped up and jittery. "I'm here now. Where's Johnson?" She raised her eyebrows impatiently.

Salvo jerked a thick thumb over his shoulder. "In the house. They're taking the fucking place apart."

"Thanks." She smacked his shoulder and took off at a jog. A porch wrapped around two sides of the house. The front door stood wide open, the screen unhooked from the closer to make it easier to carry evidence out. JT stood aside to allow an eager FBI rookie lugging two file boxes to pass. Boy, they started them younger and younger.

She slipped inside, directly into the living room. What a mess. The stink of cigarette smoke mingled with marijuana and some unidentifiable smell caught in the back of her throat.

Against one wall a stained couch sagged close to the floor. Stuffing sprouted like cauliflower from a gouge in the arm of a recliner. An end table dotted with cigarette burns was the resting place for a couple crack pipes, a syringe and a hand-held mirror coated with a white substance.

JT scanned the room for Malachuk. Her head was on his shit-list platter. If only the stakeout had remained ongoing while she dealt with Bobby and Sheets, he'd have been none the wiser.

Once they'd moved on the bust JT was screwed six ways from Tuesday. When Malachuk called as they pulled out of Gasoline Alley, he'd wanted to know "where the holy goddamn hell" she was. Then he told her in no uncertain terms he didn't care if she was crapping her pants or not, he needed all hands on deck. Said she could help search the house, and if she had to "go," she could shit behind the trees or in the cornfield. He'd said, "Buy some Immodium and don't forget toilet paper." Then he hung up on her. She'd thank Ty later for coming up with that excuse.

"Bordeaux!" Beef Hicks, a Schwarzenegger-sized black man from the Anoka County Sheriff's Department, hollered from down the hall.

JT found him in the kitchen, which was as junk-strewn as the living room. "Beef, you seen Tyrell Johnson floating around?"

"Upstairs on bedroom duty. How's the shits?" he gleefully asked, half-wedged under the sink as he worked on something. "Sucks to be you. Hey, Colombo, hand me that wrench." He nodded at a toolbox on the floor next to him. Cheryl Colombo, his Anoka County partner said, "Fuck you, Beef," and continued rifling through a drawer. Looked like they were getting along as they usually did, affection in the form of foul language.

JT handed Beef his wrench and headed for the stairway. She took them two at a time and found Tyrell exactly where Beef said he'd be, in a trashy bedroom, with clothes and garbage overtaking the bed.

He glanced up at her appearance in the doorway. "JT. I tried." He was on his knees with an arm stuffed into the side of a box spring. On the floor beside him were seven bricks of what was probably heroin.

"The shits, Ty? Really?"

"Thought it fit the stomach bug theme."

JT leaned against the doorframe. "I need another hour and that should take care of it. I've almost got my...problem... handled."

Tyrell withdrew his arm, sat back on his haunches, and studied her with a critical eye. "That 'problem' here?"

"In a matter of speaking. In the car."

"Well, Jesus. Okay. I'll tell Malachuk you came and you had to leave quick. But you better get back here fast. He's wound tighter than a helicopter pilot in a stall."

"Walk me out. If he catches sight of me we'll tell him I almost contaminated the crime scene and needed to leave and get clean clothes."

"That's disgusting. Good idea." He heaved himself to his feet and followed her out the door.

They made it to the porch. Malachuk was striding toward the house. When he caught an eyeful of who was coming out, he quickened his pace. The expression on his face was thunderous.

Tyrell muttered, "Fuckin' A." For a split second, the very space around them contracted. Then they were propelled headlong off the porch on the heels of a tremendous explosion.

The ground was still frozen, with no give when JT hit and rolled. All she could hear was a high-pitched squeal, and she didn't think her eardrums were ever going to be the same. She blinked, tried to breathe. Pushed herself to her knees. Ty. Where was Tyrell? She called out his name.

Twenty-five feet away, Malachuk swayed as he tried to right himself.

Someone hauled her to her feet. Relief burned through her when she realized Tyrell was hanging on to her. He shouted, "Find Shay!"

She could barely hear him. Thick, black smoke billowed from the front door, chasing people outside. He shoved her toward the driveway and bolted through the smoke into the house.

JT stared, mesmerized, as tendrils of flame licked the sky on the far side of the roof.

Shay. She had to get to Shay. Make sure she was okay. Then help her sisters and brothers in blue. Shouting, so much shouting, but all of it muffled and indistinct. JT ripped herself from the grim vista of the farmhouse, spun around and made a mad dash for the car.

Her girlfriend had a terrible habit of not doing what she was asked to do, and JT prayed that this one time Shay had listened. She whipped past the black SUV, and sighed in relief to see her squad. That relief lasted about two seconds. The driver's door was open. The car was empty. No Shay. No Bobby. No Sheets.

"Son of a bitch. Shay," JT tried to shout, but there was no power behind it. She cupped her hands around her mouth and tried again. Where were her wayward girlfriend and the two cons?

After making certain they weren't anywhere nearby, JT checked the multitude of emergency vehicles, the outbuildings, and then circled around the house.

As she approached the backyard, where cornstalks reflected the yellow-orange flames, the furor of the fire increased exponentially.

Flames engulfed the entire back half of the building. Part of the second story collapsed in a shower of sparks. It looked like the farmhouse had spewed all over the yard—siding, shingles, drywall, insulation, and a shitload of unidentifiable rubble littered the ground. For a moment, she flashed back to watching detritus from the Twin Towers flutter to the dust-covered pavement before the two buildings fell.

She circled the house again, helped pull from the rubble three injured cops who'd been blown out of the house and kept looking for Shay. Sirens screamed in the distance, increasing in volume as they approached the farmstead. Her hearing seemed to be coming back, but her ears hurt and her head pounded.

She made another circuit of the property, anxiety increasing with each passing minute. Around back, she followed the edge of the cornfield and scanned the debris for any signs of life.

Halfway across the yard, JT thought she caught a glint of movement. She squinted against the crap in the air. There. Was that a—yes, a hand. Fingers twitched again. It was connected to an arm that disappeared under twisted lumber and pink insulation.

She cupped her hands around her mouth and shouted, "Live one here," as she picked her way through the wreckage toward the buried body.

CHAPTER TWENTY

Something heavy held me down and everything was incredibly quiet. Half my face felt like a pincushion, and the other half felt like it was on fire. What the hell happened?

One arm was pinned to the ground by whatever was on top of me. I tried to lift the other. My muscles felt strangely weak. An orange-yellow glow reflected off my sleeve. Heat blasted the skin of my hand and I let it drop.

I rolled my head toward the source of the heat. The farmhouse, or what was left of it, was ablaze. It was kind of pretty. The flames were mesmerizing. I thought I should wonder where the second story went, but the flickering light was entirely too fascinating to care.

The ground was cold. Really cold. The iciness seeped into my back and butt and calves. It felt like I was in the cellar again, but I wasn't. I could feel my toes but my legs were pinned and I couldn't pull them out from whatever they were under.

What was I doing here? Chasing someone. Sheets. And Bobby. Around the yard. The farmhouse was on fire. I was so tired.

I closed my eyes.

Something touched my forehead. I blinked. Blinked again. JT was looking down at me. Her eyes were wide. A terrified expression twisted her face. Her mouth opened and closed and her eyes got wider. Her face was smudged with something black.

"What?" That might have been more of a croak than a word. Why did my voice sound so loud in my head?

My lover gestured wildly, and then someone pulled her away.

* * *

Sometime later, the strobing red and blue and white lights had multiplied with the addition of a whole bunch of emergency vehicles.

I sat in the back of an ambulance, wrapped in a blanket after being subjected to a whole lot of pokes and prods and lights in my eyes. JT was perched on the narrow rolling bed beside me with an arm around my shoulders, which was deceiving. On the outside she looked like a caring girlfriend while in reality she was simply making sure I couldn't bolt.

I hadn't been super fond of the medical profession since the accident and subsequent surgeries I'd had when I was a kid.

She'd wiped most of the black soot off her face and didn't look quite so scary. The sleeve of her jacket had a six-inch slice, and her forearm was wrapped in white bandages.

Everything sounded far away, kind of echo-y, as if Rocky had stuffed cotton balls in my ears as a joke. For the most part I was slowly beginning to hear what people were saying, so I figured that was a good sign.

They'd wanted to transport me to the hospital as soon as a substantial part of the wall and a very dead Dwight Sheets were lifted off me, but I refused to go. The paramedics ascertained I didn't have a spinal injury and after I tried to get up myself, they trundled my ass to an ambulance parked in the back half of the yard.

Things slowly began coming back as I tried to remain still for a paramedic friend of JT's who was working on removing embedded glass from my cheek. Bobby and Sheets. Their escape from the car. The chase around the back of the house. My tackle, which threw Sheets off-balance and probably saved my life. A piece of flying rebar had pierced his chest like an arrow.

"Ow!" I jerked away from the patient hand of the medic, whose name was Patty something. I'd met her a few times, and liked her well enough. She made me laugh. Her last name reminded me of Bam Bam. Sham? Spam? Schramm. That was it.

"Stop it, Shay," she said. She sure wasn't making me laugh now. "You don't behave, I'm going to haul your dirty behind to the hospital whether you like it or not. Don't even tempt me."

I frowned, but stopped as tweezers pulled away glass near the corner of my eye.

Tyrell jogged up, concern etched on his face, made darker yet by the soot covering every inch of him. "How's she coming?" He looked about as good as JT, which was to say, frightening. The white shirt under his leather jacket was grimy. One of his eyebrows had been singed, and his pants were ripped. I thought I saw blood on his neck. He gave me a once-over. "Can't stay out of trouble, can you?"

I gave him the side eye without moving my head. "No. Are we done yet, Patty?"

"Nope." Her tone was way too cheerful. No one should be that cheerful while they dissected someone's cheek.

"If you'd sit still she could finish," JT said.

"You try not moving when someone's playing with glass protruding from your face," I retorted then yelped, "OW!" I glared at Patty, who triumphantly held up a shard the size of my thumbnail.

She said, "You're lucky this wasn't a quarter inch to the right or you'd be down an eye." She dropped the fragment into a red biohazard container.

"Any luck finding Bobby Temple, Ty?" JT asked.

"No. I think six or seven suspects hit the cornfields and are in the wind. Maybe him too. Shay mentioned he was running closer to the field than the house. They're still looking."

His already bass voice deepened, making it even harder for me to hear. "It looks like we lost two, six seriously injured. None of those injuries are life-threatening."

My hearing hadn't improved but I didn't miss that. Holy Mahoney.

"Jesus." JT rubbed her temples. "Who? Were they task force or regular LE?"

For a second Tyrell didn't speak. "Ours. Hicks and Columbo. They were in the kitchen when it blew." Ty swallowed hard enough I could see his Adam's apple bob beneath his skin. He blinked rapidly, then looked at me. "You and Sheets were outside the kitchen window when the explosive detonated. That's where the glass you're modeling came from. It's a miracle you weren't killed too."

"Son of a—" JT's breath hitched, and she covered her face with a hand. A second later she dropped it, her eyes glittering like granite. "Anything left in there we can use? Or was this whole shitstorm for nothing?"

"Most of the damage is limited to the back of the house. Firefighters got things under control before the whole thing went up."

Patty asked, "What caused the explosion?"

"No idea yet," Tyrell said. "They were searching the kitchen when one of the guys saw Columbo open a hatch to a small compartment by the back door. Bang."

"Yee-ouch!" I glared at Patty as she dropped another shard in the container. "Aren't you done yet?"

She gave me the skank eye, which was so effective I wondered if she'd learned it from Eddy. "One more to go and I think you'll be good. Hold still, for chrissake."

Patty extracted the last of it, and then swabbed my face with a cotton ball soaked in some kind of smelly goop and then added a few butterfly strips. "Go," she said, "Before I change my mind." Her gentle touch outweighed the brusqueness of her tone.

"Thanks, Patty," JT said. "I'll take this one home. Ty, I'll check in later, okay?"

"No sweat." He ruffled the hair on the top of my head. "Be a good girl now or JT will tell Daddy."

I flipped him the bird and handed the blanket to Patty. "Thanks."

She clobbered me on the shoulder. "Anytime. Well, hopefully never again, but you know what I mean."

JT jumped to the ground and helped me down. My feet hit gravel and the world tilted. I squawked and JT grabbed my arm. Earlier Patty had told us a person's balance involved the inner ear, and right now mine was not performing up to optimal standards.

"Hey, JT," Patty called, "don't forget to make her an appointment with an ear, nose and throat doc."

"Got it." JT gave Patty a wave and slid a steadying arm around me.

It took forever to shuffle across the circular drive to JT's squad. Once she buckled me in and started the car, she gripped the steering wheel and stared straight ahead for a few long seconds. Finally she turned to face me, her midnight eyes snapping with fury.

"Don't you dare do that to me ever again, Shay Elizabeth O'Hanlon. I thought you were dead."

Then she did something I'd never seen her do. She burst into tears.

CHAPTER TWENTY-ONE

Doctor Beth approached the examination table. I eyed her warily as she pulled a hand-held torture device from the pocket of her white jacket. A stethoscope hung around her neck, and the over-bright fluorescent light reflected off its metal parts.

JT sat on a chair beside the narrow ledge they called a desk. "Shay, she's only going to look in your ears."

The words were still muffled, but less so. My vertigo had all but disappeared. I really hoped those were good signs.

I flinched when Beth reached for my ear.

"For Pete's sake, Shay," Beth said. "It's an otoscope—a flashlight and magnifying lenses with a bendable head—if that makes you feel better. All it does is allow me to see into your ear canal. Just like I've done every other time you've been in here. Now hold still."

For the last twenty years Beth had cared for Eddy, Coop and me, but I tried to make it a point not to come calling more often than for my yearly checkup. Beth knew what happened to me all those years ago—she'd taken a look at my abdomen during one of those first visits and we'd become friends over conversations revolving around what surgeries I'd had and what recovery protocols I'd followed. I shied away from most things medical, and while Beth no longer treated me with kid gloves, she knew sometimes just doing instead of asking permission got the job done. JT had caught onto that pretty quick too.

She tilted my head and stuck the black, funnel-shaped thingie in my ear, which didn't hurt but felt weirder than usual. I tried to behave when she circled the table and repeated the procedure on the other side.

"See," she said, "not so bad." She turned off the light and dropped the instrument into the pocket of her coat. A warm hand cupped my chin and she inspected my face. "JT, looks like that paramedic friend of yours did a good job getting the glass out. Most of the cuts aren't too deep, but the one by your eye might leave a half-inch scar. You were really lucky." She stepped back. "You can get down now."

I hopped off the table and took a seat next to JT. Beth leaned against the exam table and crossed her arms. "Both eardrums have small perforations, but nothing, I think, that won't heal with time."

Whew.

"Is there anything she should be doing?" JT asked.

"No loud noises until everything's healed. That means no concerts. Don't take her to the shooting range with you. Shay, if we get a last blast of snow and you use the snowblower, make sure you wear the earmuffs you use when you go to the range. Otherwise, that's about it. Unless something changes, come back and see me if things aren't back to normal in six weeks. And mind you, it might take longer than that to heal fully but it doesn't mean anything is seriously wrong."

We thanked Beth and left.

The clinic was two blocks away from my favorite ice cream joint, and I was feeling sorry for myself. "Since I'm injured and all, how about some Sebastian Joe's? Ice cream always makes me feel better."

"Of course it does." JT's tone was sarcastic, but the corner of her mouth lifted in amusement. "Let's go."